THE COVERED BRIDGE

By Cornelia Meigs

THE COVERED BRIDGE
WIND IN THE CHIMNEY
MASTER SIMON'S GARDEN
AS THE CROW FLIES
THE NEW MOON
THE POOL OF STARS
THE WINDY HILL
RAIN ON THE ROOF
THE WONDERFUL LOCOMOTIVE
THE WILLOW WHISTLE
THE KINGDOM OF THE WINDING ROAD
HELGA AND THE WHITE PEACOCK (A Play)
THE STEADFAST PRINCESS (A Play)

THE
COVERED
BRIDGE

BY CORNELIA MEIGS

ILLUSTRATED BY
MARGUERITE DE ANGELI

NEW YORK

The Macmillan Company

1937

PRINTED IN THE UNITED STATES OF AMERICA
BY THE STRATFORD PRESS, INC., NEW YORK

To the good Vermont friends
who have made this story
possible

Contents

Illustrations

THE COVERED BRIDGE

I

Portrait of Peter

THE CANDLES on the supper table had begun to blink and waver a little before Connie's very sleepy eyes, but a word that Uncle Roger let fall startled her into complete wakefulness again. She had come on a journey that day, all the way from Gloucester, jolting in the coach over the muddy roads to Boston, so that it was no wonder that her eyes drooped a little before the long meal was over. Great silver dishes were set down before Uncle Roger and then taken away again by Thompson, the man who waited on the table; plates were changed solemnly over and over. Constance was not used to meals that were so carefully served and that took so long to eat.

She was so tired that she was just wondering if she might ask her aunt if she could be excused, when Uncle Roger said, "Yes, it's a very fine plan, but what shall we do about Constance?"

She sat up very straight then, to hear what would come next.

Aunt Clarissa, at the other end of the table, did not answer at once and then at last she said, "Constance, dear, wouldn't you like to take your little cake in your hand and go out into the kitchen to talk to Sarah? This has been a long supper at the end of a long day. Sarah will go upstairs with you when you are ready to go to bed."

There was really nothing at all that Connie could do but say, "Yes, Aunt Clarissa," very politely, as her mother had told her to be so careful to do, and get down with her round cake held in her hand.

Thompson pulled out her chair for her. She did not really want to go; she was anxious, as anyone might be, to hear what they were going to do "about Constance."

The kitchen, however, with its big fire and the comfortable-sounding clock ticking on the wall, looked very cozy and cheerful to a slightly homesick little girl whose mother and father had sailed away on his ship for a voyage to the West Indies, a little girl who had come, for the first time, to visit Uncle Roger and Aunt Clarissa. In the year seventeen hundred and eighty-eight, voyages to the West Indies and back took several months, and Connie's visit to Boston was to last for all that time.

Sarah Macomber, who had cooked the supper and was now waiting for it to be over, was sitting by the fire knitting. The moment Connie came into the kitchen, her eye fell upon something that was hanging on the wall below the clock, something so surprising that she asked at once, before Sarah could speak, "What's that?"

Sarah looked up from her knitting and answered calmly, "Oh, that's Peter."

Constance came across to look more closely at this very strange likeness. It was a big, stiff sheet of paper cut out in the shape of a boy, a rather short, squarish boy who had evidently lain down on the floor for someone to draw around him. His arms and legs were stretched out and the back of his head had touched the paper so little that it looked very small. It was just the sort of shape, Connie thought at once, that you make when you lie down to print your figure in the snow. But this one had been cut out and hung up against the whitewashed wall.

"There's another one," said Sarah, "beyond the door. And the third one is over next to the cupboard."

[2]

The second record of Peter was bigger, with longer legs and broader shoulders. And the one beside the cupboard was the biggest of all.

Connie asked in wonder, "What makes you have such queer pictures of Peter?"

"Why," returned Sarah placidly, "because people like me, who have little money to spare, can't have pictures in the usual way of those they love. Peter is my grandson, the only one I have. He is twelve years old, and a big boy now. He has come to stay with me for a month every year while your uncle and aunt go traveling in the South. This year I'm going to him."

"And how does he get here?" Connie asked.

"He comes all the way from Vermont in the coach. I live in Vermont, too, in Hebron, in the Green Mountains. I sometimes feel very far from home in this city by the sea. When Peter is big enough to earn our living, or when I am too old to make it anymore, then we are going to live together. We talk about it, over and over. He stays with some cousins; for he has no mother and father. It is always hard for both of us when he has to go away from me; that is why he thought of leaving me his picture."

As Connie listened, her heart went back to the moment when she had said good-by to her father and mother yesterday, and how her father had said that a ship captain's daughter must be brave because there was nothing else to be. For a second it seemed almost as though she couldn't be brave a minute longer, then suddenly, in answer to Sarah's understanding smile, and because she could not speak, she sat down on the floor beside the bench and put her cheek against Sarah's smooth linen apron.

"There now," Sarah was saying, while her hand stroked Connie's

[3]

yellow hair, "you know there's worse things than having our dear ones go away, when we know they will soon come back again."

Connie turned her head sideways against Sarah's knee and looked up into the kind face above her. It was an odd face, with its fine little lines, its very dark blue eyes and crinkled gray hair. Sarah Macomber might sit in the kitchen and cook for Aunt Clarissa, but she was a person, an unusual person, just the same.

Constance began to explain to Sarah about what had been said in the dining room. Everything had been settled, it seemed, for her to spend these months of the winter with her aunt and uncle, but just an hour or two ago Uncle Roger had got a business letter that called him to South Carolina and would keep him there a great many weeks. Aunt Clarissa would go with him, she always did. They would be moving from one place to another and there would be no school for Connie to go to. They had promised that she should go to school. So they were wondering "what is to be done with Connie." The little girl was wondering herself, even more anxiously than Uncle Roger could be. "They are talking about it now," she finished. "Oh, what do you think they will decide?"

Sarah sat very still for a few minutes, her face puckering, as Connie was to learn that it always did when she was thinking hard. Her blue eyes looked straight before her at the likeness of Peter on the wall. Suddenly, very suddenly, she got up and put out her hand to Connie. All she said was, "Come with me now, and we will go in and talk to them."

The candles were still bright on the dining-room table and Thompson was just setting out the tiny gold-colored coffee cups. Uncle Roger looked a trifle troubled and Aunt Clarissa even seemed worried too, as though their talk had not got them anywhere near to solving the problem that had to do with their nine-year-old niece, Constance Anderson. Sarah stood respectfully in the doorway, waiting for them to ask her to come in, but it seemed very plain that she was as important a person as anyone else in the room. Aunt Clarissa gave her a little nod. "Yes, Sarah, what is it?"

Sarah took Connie's hand firmly in hers and came forward into the circle of candlelight. She spoke very quietly, but with the sure tone of that special sort of person who knows her own mind. "I think you have been worrying about what is to become of the little young lady, if you must go away. I have an idea. Why should she not come with me, back to the farm in the mountains? Every child does well for living on a farm some time. And a mountain farm is like no other. If she goes with me that will settle everything."

"But that part of Vermont is new rough country, only just beginning to be settled," Uncle Roger objected. "How will she go to school?"

Aunt Clarissa added, "Up there in the mountains it is so bitterly cold." She gave a little shiver that fluttered her lace ruffles.

"There'll be no trouble about schools," Sarah answered. "She will be safe and well, too, and maybe less lonely than here in a city where she knows nobody. And as for the cold, there's fires and cloaks and muffs and fur-lined hoods will keep that out."

Aunt Clarissa answered quickly and gaily, "It's like you, Sarah Macomber, to think of a way out for us all. Constance, would you like to go with Sarah, child?"

"Oh, I would," Connie cried at once. She could not have explained why, but she felt that Sarah was the sort of person she could go with anywhere.

Uncle Roger leaned back in his chair and drew a long breath that sounded like a sigh of relief. "I make you my compliments, Sarah. There's some wisdom in the plan. But we won't decide too quickly. Let the child be sure she wants to go."

Half an hour later Connie was going to bed in the big chintz-curtained room on the third floor. Sarah had come up to help her find what she needed and to see that she was well cared for. It was a pleasant room with wide windows and a high carved bed, hung with its flowered curtains.

Sarah tucked in the soft down coverlid and said seriously, "You will have no such room as this, or any such bed, if you come to the farm to stay with me, my dear. And there will be real work that you and I will have to do together, for it is no small thing to take care of a farmhouse through the winter. It is not too late to ask your aunt and uncle to let you go with them if you would rather. The truth is that they do not quite know what to do about a little girl your size and just how to make her happy. They love you. They mean to be kind."

Connie did not answer at once, as she sat up among the fat white pillows and looked at the fire dwindling to coals below the white mantel. Yes, she was thinking, her aunt and uncle meant to be kind. But Sarah knew how to be kind. That was all the difference. "I want to go with you," she said.

The room seemed to be bright, suddenly, with Sarah's warm, delighted smile. "That is good," she answered. "I want you to come. You will be a real help to me, for we will have much to do, between us. I am going to depend on you, Constance."

She had called her Miss Constance in the beginning, Connie remembered, but she evidently did not intend to anymore. It was as though they were already partners in the new venture.

[6]

It was a long journey to go by coach, into western Massachusetts and then up into Vermont, through the chilly October weather. Connie loved every mile of it, the hill roads, the brooks tumbling down to meet them, the little inns where they slept at night. Everyone seemed to know Sarah, wherever they stopped.

Sarah knitted as she sat on the jolting seat of the coach beside Connie, and her mind seemed as busy with plans as her fingers were with her needles. She seemed to grow younger and gayer with every mile they traveled. She explained to Connie how she and her husband, Jonathan Macomber, had owned the farm on the hill above a town named Hebron, a farm where she had lived for all her married life. "We came early to that new country, and it was hard toil for both of us, who had grown up in the ease and convenience of a city like Boston. But we both loved the land; our people had been farmers before us and the feeling for it was in our bones."

At the time when her husband died, a debt had been laid on the land, and Sarah could not rest until it was all repaid. So she had gone back to Boston, to find work with Connie's Aunt Clarissa. "But I have put by enough money now to pay it all," she ended, "and the next thing is to think about the farm again, for that needs me. A farm must not be left alone, or it will turn back into wilderness. Jonathan worked so hard for it that I can never let that happen. It had been in my mind for some days to tell your aunt that it was time for me to go back, but I had not quite got to the point of saying it. But, when I saw your need, I knew, all in a minute, what we must do."

She looked very pretty, sitting there, explaining her affairs to Connie, wrapped in her figured shawl and wearing a bonnet with a rose in it. In her own sedate, gray-haired way, she was as good to look upon as pretty, fashionable Aunt Clarissa. When a big man in a rough gray overcoat got into the coach at a crossroads stop, and hailed her with loud welcome, she seemed to glow with excitement and pleasure.

"I've come home for good, Cousin Cephas," she told him. "Now I can really take care of the place as I have long wanted to do. I'm going to have twice as many fowls as I used to, and a new hen house—" She began explaining her plans so fast that she was breathless.

"Ay, that's good," Cephas answered, "but what of the little young lady here? She has not just the look of farming folk. Is she going to be content with all this?"

"Oh yes," Connie answered him shyly. She loved animals and all live things. "I'm to carry water and feed to the chickens every morning."

Cephas' face, which had that same kind, friendly look that Sarah's had, grew a little grave, then suddenly brightened. "I was thinking it might be lonely for her, but I know just the thing. We have five puppies at our house, children of our old gray-and-white sheep dog Martha. Would the child like one? They're good company, and are useful when they grow big. If she'd like to have it, she can get down when the coach stops near my house, and then walk up the hill to yours. I will put her on her way over the bridge."

Connie and Sarah agreed gladly. They would both love to have the dog. "We'll be there very soon," Cousin Cephas said.

The coach had climbed very high now, but there still towered above the road a great brown hill with all its slopes streaked with the snow wreaths of late October. When the door of the coach opened there blew in a cold freshness that was like nothing else that

"I've come home for good, Cousin Cephas," she told him.

Constance had ever known, even though it reminded her a little of wind off the sea. Cousin Cephas got ready to climb out and Connie got up to follow him.

"Don't be long," Sarah directed. "I will need you, don't forget."

The young sheep dogs all came running to meet them, round bundles of gray fur, with broad friendly faces and dark eyes almost hidden by their bushy hair. They had strong round hindquarters and no tails at all. Connie spent a long time choosing one, now and then forgetting all about a choice just for the pleasure of playing with them.

Cousin Cephas said once or twice, "You really should make haste. There's a look of snow in those clouds and Sarah will be waiting."

But Connie had never liked to make haste. She chose, at last, the darkest gray puppy with a white spot on his shoulder and a knowing white face. She would have stayed to romp with them a little longer, had not Cousin Cephas' red-cheeked wife spoken firmly from the doorway. "You must come in and drink a cup of milk, child, and then you must go on. Sarah may be anxious if you wait any longer."

Cousin Cephas brought a strap and a cord so that Constance could lead the dog, but the puppy seemed happy enough to go with her and kept rubbing against her knees and wagging contentedly, even though it was himself he wagged, for want of a tail.

"His name is Jock," Cephas told her.

They set out along the road, all three together.

All along the journey, especially as they began to get into the hill country, the coach had rumbled over one bridge after another, crossing streams without number. Most of the bridges had walls and roofs like houses. Their board floors were soft with gathered dust, and there were glimpses, now and then, of the streams rushing be-

[11]

low, seen through slits between the boards of the wall. They came to one now, with a clear brown brook running below it.

"Why do they make tops on bridges, like this?" Connie asked as they walked across together, with Jock trailing behind to sniff in the corners of the big, jutting beams. He was plainly a dog full of curiosity.

Cousin Cephas explained about covered bridges. "The rain might rot the boards of the floor, and we like our bridges to last a hundred years or so at least. We build them high, so that the floods can't reach them, and we roof them over to shed the rain. This one has stood here a long time. The stream is Hebron Brook and it divides these three upper farms from those like mine, which are lower down the valley. Sarah's place is the first one above. Now that's your way up the lane. Go right straight up the hill, and you'll have plenty of time to get to the house before the snow begins." He turned about and left her.

The coach road wound away to curve out of sight around the mountain; but Connie's way was up the narrower lane, plainly marked between two stone walls. She began to climb upward and then stopped to look back. How high she was! She could look down on the whole long valley, dotted with white houses and big red barns, marked by the windings of the road and the more crooked turnings of Hebron Brook. She had never been so far from any house before, had never stood alone on a hill like that, feeling that the whole world was at her feet. That strangely fresh, cold air filled her lungs and made her cheeks glow red. She was bold, excited, laughing.

Jock gave a sudden twitch at the cord and jerked it out of her hand. He had sniffed a rabbit and went bounding away from her, over the wall, straight up the side of the hill. She ran after him; she wanted to see the rabbit too. They could not get near it, but she stopped to pick some wintergreen berries, showing red at the edge of a wreath of hard snow. She and Jock ran and scampered, stopped to catch their breath, and ran again.

Suddenly she stood still. The air was getting colder; something fluttered past her face; something chilly touched her cheek. It was beginning to snow. And Cousin Cephas had said they must go right up the lane to the house and she had forgotten it.

What was it that Sarah had said, the evening that Connie had made her choice to go with her? "I am going to depend on you, Constance." But Connie was not being dependable now, not at all. She had yet to learn that in these far, high places of the world, where there are not many neighbors about, people have to be dependable, have to do what they say they will. Otherwise things go wrong. She did not know it yet, but she began to feel it suddenly. The snow was coming down faster.

She was off the path and it took her some little time to get back to it. There was even one horrid second, just a little one, when she thought she could not find it. But Jock would have, if she could not. He nosed and sniffed and went steadily down the slope until they were in the lane again. The snow was like a white curtain about them, a thin curtain through which she could see the bushes and the trees close by, but which hid the valley as though it had never been. She liked the snow, she was not frightened, she was only sorry that Sarah must be waiting. Sarah had got off the coach at the foot of the hill and had walked up alone, carrying the bags and bundles. Connie had not thought of that. She pressed forward.

The flakes fell so fast that the ground was already white and beginning to be slippery underfoot. She could not walk as quickly as

[13]

she wanted to. Jock gave up dashing ahead and tugging at the cord, and now came plodding along at her heels. Finally he sat down and whimpered. He was only a baby after all, and he was very tired. She gathered him up in her arms, although he was heavy and wet and she could hardly keep her balance. Still she pushed on.

"There is nothing to be frightened about," her mind kept telling her steadily as she toiled along. She was a little girl, climbing a hill to a house where someone who loved her was waiting for her. But the hill was a mountain and the house was one she had never seen. That made it a little different.

Jock yelped suddenly and wriggled so that she had to put him down. She saw why in a moment—they were coming to the house. Sarah had told her about it so many times that Connie could never have failed to know it, a low roof, a row of windows looking out toward the valley, the long line of the ell behind, and the big, square chimney in the middle.

"Sarah," she called, "I'm here." Now Sarah need not be anxious about her anymore.

But no one answered. Connie came close. There was light behind the windows, a moving light of the kind that comes from a fire on the hearth. But the snow was smooth over the ground before the house, with only a single footprint on the doorstep. She looked more closely yet. What was this mark in the snow, on the white surface below the eaves where the flakes had drifted in and fallen more gently and were slower in covering up anything that was to be seen there? And what did she see? A shape printed in the snow, a body with arms and legs stretched out, the figure of a boy, tall, but still rather squarely built.

[14]

"Why," she cried out aloud, "it's Peter. I didn't know that Peter was going to be here."

She ran to the door. It opened under her hand and she stood still in a big low-ceilinged room, with a bright fire burning in the stone chimney place, with a red cover on the table and plates and bowls set out on it. But there was nobody there.

II

Nicodemus

IT WAS fortunate that the sheep-dog puppy was wet with snow and whimpering. This was his usual supper time, and five minutes of waiting will make a puppy think he is starved. Constance, feeling perfectly bewildered by the surprise of coming into an empty house where she had expected to find Sarah, still was sure that she ought not to let the dog be anxious too. She set Jock down by the fire and told him to be quiet and good, while she looked for something to eat. He lay down with his paws out before him and watched her with quiet bright eyes, evidently quite sure that she would know what to do.

And, surprisingly, Connie did. Never before had she had a kitchen to herself and a hungry mouth to fill, but quite to her own astonishment she found herself bringing out a crock of milk, getting down a little iron pan with three short legs and putting it among the hot coals at the edge of the fire with the milk in it. She spilled a little on the clean hearth, but Jock licked it up promptly. She found a crusty loaf of bread on the pantry shelf, covered up with a red and white napkin. Not for a moment did she stop to wonder how such things had got so quickly into a house that had been long closed. It was almost like one of the fairy tales in which the princess is served by unseen hands in the enchanted castle. She did not feel at all like a princess, however; she enjoyed, much more, feeling capable and

She enjoyed feeling capable and powerful, able to take care of herself and Jock.

powerful, able to take care of herself and Jock. It was just as Jock was lapping the last tongueful of milk from the bottom of his bowl that there was a bustle at the back door, and a sound of voices, and Sarah came in.

The wind had blown through her crinkly hair, and her cheeks were a brighter pink, even, than they had been in the coach. She looked back over her shoulder and announced, "Yes, it's all right. She's here and she's even known how to find the dog his supper."

Someone came in over the low step behind her, a taller someone than Connie had expected, with the wind in his hair, too, as it stood out around his head. His eyes were very bright and his face was freckled. It was Peter.

There was a great deal of laughter and talk and explaining over the supper which they all got ready together. Fortunately, no one asked Constance to explain one thing, how she had managed to spend so much time coming up the hill. What they had to tell one another was how Sarah had not been sure that the cousin with whom Peter had been living would be willing to spare him on such short notice, therefore Sarah had not spoken to Connie about his coming, for fear of disappointment. But the cousins had said that of course Peter must be with his grandmother, and so he had come up a few days before and, with the help of Cousin Margaret, the fair-haired wife of Cousin Cephas, had got the house clean and the fires going. Cousin Margaret had baked bread and fried doughnuts and aired the blankets, so that everything would be ready.

"But why—why—?" Constance began. Sarah answered before she had finished.

"Why were we both out when you came? Why, Peter has four calves, his very own, that are going to live in the barn this winter.

They were out in the pasture and we had to get them in when we saw that the snow was coming."

When Connie went to bed that night it was in a room very different indeed from the one she had slept in at her aunt's house. It was a little one off Sarah's, with a sloping ceiling and a bed so high that one had to step on a footstool to climb into it. Besides this, it was made higher yet by the pile of feather beds and patchwork quilts which covered it, topped by a gay blue and white knitted cover which Connie seemed to recognize. "Why, you were knitting this the night I came to Boston."

"Yes," Sarah answered, "even when you are away from a farmhouse you can always be doing things for it."

Jock settled down by the fireplace where there was a flicker of fire still. "I'll put back the curtain," Sarah said, when Connie was all tucked in against the cold, "so that you can see when the morning comes."

She took away the candle, and Connie could see from her bed the big mountains looming against the sky even in the dark, and the sheet of snow lying lightly over everything and making the night less black. She dropped into slumber and wakened some time later, when the log on the hearth fell in two with a little crash and a shower of sparks. The storm had cleared, and the moon was shining in the bright sky opposite her window. She sat up as best she could under the mountain of covers and looked out at the still, empty beauty of the great hills and long slopes, all softly clear in the moonlight. She was smiling to herself, she did not quite know why, when she snuggled down under the quilts again and fell deeply asleep.

It was Sarah's coming in to make the fire that woke her. Connie felt a little ashamed to be waited on like that, but Sarah did all her work so easily and happily that one never could feel that such kind care was a burden. "It's going to be a fine day," Sarah told her, "not really winter yet at all. When the fire burns up brightly, then it will be time to get up. Make haste and dress. Peter wants to show you something."

When they all three came outdoors after their breakfast in front of the fire, their breath went up like steam in the clear, frosty morning. The thin covering of hard snow crackled under their feet. Peter had run ahead and let his four calves out of the barn. They were bigger than Connie had expected, as large as good-sized ponies, and so full of gay spirits that they simply could not keep their hind feet on the ground. They were black, or black and white, strong, sturdy little beasts, who ran and capered, making it hard to decide whether they were chasing Peter or he was running after them. He let down the bars of the barnyard gate and they went galloping away up the hill, while he trudged behind them carrying a bucket. Connie looked questioningly at the coarse white stuff which filled it.

"That's salt," Peter told her briefly. He was apt to use very few words, Connie had already discovered, but his wide, quick smile made up for all he did not say. It was plain from his sagging shoulders that the bucket was heavy. Connie sidled closer and took hold of the handle to help him. He smiled down at her; he did not say that he didn't need any help. She liked that. Yes, she and Peter were going to be friends.

They had reached a high shoulder of the hill. Constance looked back and caught her breath. How far, how very far one could see, how tiny was the world below, how clean and tingling was the air.

She could know from Sarah's bright face how she, too, loved the great wide view of mountainside and far valley. Connie stood looking and looking, until Sarah touched her arm.

"Watch," Sarah said. Jock, who had come panting behind, sat down beside her as they stood still.

Peter was spreading out the salt over the surface of a flat rock which he had cleaned of snow. Now, when the bucket was empty, he climbed up on a big stone and put his hands to each side of his mouth, took a deep breath and began to call, "Come, doddy. Come, doddy. Co-o-me." He stopped for breath and then began again, "Come—come."

Connie did not know what to expect. Then she began to see them come, the black cattle which were pastured all over the mountainside. Some were young and active, as gay as Peter's calves and perhaps not many months older. They came galloping out of the woods and over the hill, almost as swift and easily moving as deer. The older animals followed, sleek mothers with partly grown sons and daughters beside them, and young bulls with bushy forelocks. They gathered from every direction; those who had been beyond the reach of Peter's call saw the others running and ran too.

They began to collect around the flat rock, shy at first and eying the three warily. Peter they knew, but Constance was strange and so was Jock. Their big eyes rolled; their broad ears twitched; they put out long curling tongues to touch the salt they loved and then drew back, not quite sure of themselves. Constance had pushed close to Sarah, since a ring of forty or fifty large black cattle is a little frightening. The crowd parted and the big bull, the master of the herd, came shouldering through. He was so huge that not even Sarah could have looked over his back; his head looked small in proportion to his enormous shoulders, and his long face was smooth and black, so black as to be almost blue. He might have seemed a terrible thing, but as Connie moved quickly to draw even closer to Sarah, he in his turn jumped back, startled.

"Why," she exclaimed, "he's afraid of me." And she burst out laughing. And then as she looked at his broad face and big soft eyes she had an odd feeling the big bull looked kind.

The others came pushing up now, the boldest ones began to lick up the salt, the others followed. The great bull—his name, Peter told her, was Nicodemus—dropped his head and took his own share, a surprisingly small one considering his great size, then moved away to make room for the rest. They none of them had horns, only wide, alert black ears that stood out from their beautifully shaped heads. Their eyes were as black as their smooth dark hair, but showed rolling glimpses of white as they glanced up, nervously and timidly still, at so terrible a stranger as Constance. She reached out and patted one wide forehead; another was pushed forward to be patted also.

"Take care," Peter warned. "Stand well up on the stone. They are big and clumsy and might push you over, just trying to get close to you. So, doddy, so. Go back, my beauties." He was masterful with them, as though they were all his own.

They drew back, and began to wander away, having got their taste of the salt which all cattle need and have to be given at intervals. Peter picked up the empty bucket, and swinging it gaily, set off down the hill. Jock had sat very sedately on the stone, watching them. Cows were his business, of course. He must already feel that in his bones, but he did not know much about them yet. As he came scampering after them, one of the half-grown calves got in his way and he made a little dash at it, whereat the big creature turned aside.

[23]

Jock stood still, looking most surprised that so large a beast would pay any attention to him.

"Quick," said Peter.

Another of the bigger calves was dashing down headlong and about to blunder into a little steep-sided hollow, with rocky sides. Peter turned him back, Jock running and barking and helping him. The puppy came wagging up, very triumphant with his first success.

"He's going to learn to drive cattle easily enough," Peter declared, patting him. "That hollow is a bad place for an animal to slip into when he's running. In a month he'll be taking the calves out to the watering trough. We won't ever again have the chase after them that we had last night."

There was something in Connie's mind. It had lain there heavily ever since the evening before, a rankling thing that was growing large and troublesome, as a grievance always does. Would she have the courage to speak out about it to Peter? That half-hour in the field seemed to have made them close friends. Yes, she would ask him before the thought began to get any worse.

"Don't you think," she began, "that it's a little queer when a person comes to your house—a person from a long way off—don't you think it's just—not quite right for everyone to be away when she gets there?"

"But," said Peter, not in the least astonished, only explaining what was so clear to him, "but we were out getting the calves in."

"Yes." Connie was a persistent person. She was going to get to the end of the matter this time. "But calves are—are just animals and people are—they're people."

Little girls were people, that was what she was trying to tell him. She did not like to think that just because she was a little girl they would have neglected her. Peter seemed to understand fully, for he thought about it gravely for a long minute. He seemed to know the answer to her question but not to be able to put it exactly into words. At last he could say it.

"Of course people are the most important, but you have to think about animals too. When animals are wild they can take care of themselves, but if you take them and use them you owe them something. You shut them up inside of gates, and in pastures, so they can't get to shelter if there's a storm, or any such things. So you have to see that they do. It wouldn't be fair if you didn't."

Connie walked along for some time pondering this idea. Yes, it really was true. You owed something to the animals, if you made them help you instead of helping themselves. Jock was walking very soberly beside her as though he, too, was thinking over just what his duty was in this new business of taking care of a farm. Then he spied a chipmunk, sitting on a stone, at just the same moment that Connie and Peter did. They all three went racing after it, even though each one of them—even Jock—knew that long before they could reach the place it would whisk into its hole, with a saucy flirt of its tail.

Sarah had been following more slowly behind. When they got to the house, she gave Connie her first lesson in feeding the chickens, how to keep from scattering the food over the backs of the crowding creatures, how to make sure the smaller ones got what they needed when the bigger, greedier ones tried to push them aside.

"And you must hurry a little," Sarah explained, as Connie would have spent a far longer time over the fowls' breakfast, "or there won't be enough time left for you to get to school."

"School," echoed Connie. "Am I going to school right now, this very day?"

"Why yes," Sarah answered. "The term has begun. There is no reason to wait. Peter is going, and the children from the Guyers' house, up the hill. They expect to stop for you."

It was only a minute later that Connie looked out of the window and saw what must be the Guyer children, although they looked to her like a troop of brownies. There were six of them, in brown coats; the girls had hoods and the boys woolen caps pulled down over their ears. One had a gay green scarf and another bright red mittens and one, curiously enough, had a knitted muffler of blue and white, just like that out of which Sarah had knitted the cover for Connie's bed. They did not look in the least alike, some faces were broad, some narrow, some eyes were blue and dancing and at least one pair was dark and thoughtful. And what was so very odd was that several of them looked as though they were about the same age. There was no time to ask questions, however, she must hurry to put on her cloak and set off with them.

The way led down the lane, across the covered bridge, and along a path to the schoolhouse, set back from the road in a clump of tall butternut trees. It was a very small schoolhouse indeed, with wide windows looking toward the brook and up the side of the mountain. The schoolmaster was a middle-aged, quiet man, with a bush of gray hair and a bright, absent-minded smile, as though most of the time he was thinking of something very far removed from the long room and the twelve rosy faces set in rows before him. He gave Connie a place beside the window, with Dinah, the oldest, brown-haired Guyer girl beside her.

"You will have to move closer to the fire when the weather begins to grow cold," the schoolmaster said, "but just now I know you want to get acquainted with the brook."

She did get acquainted with it. Long after, Connie looked back on this thing or that which she had learned in that school, and found the memory always mingled with the sound of rushing water, which came in even with the window closed; with the sight of gray rocks marked with patterns of moss and, above them, a long upward slope of stony ground scattered over with slim, supple, white birch trees. She learned the multiplication table to the tune of the splashing of Hebron Brook, and the sound of it always went through her head when she thought of six times eight are forty-eight, six times nine are fifty-four.

When Connie got home she was so full of questions that she was asking them until the very moment when she climbed into bed. The last one was, "Do all those beautiful black cows belong to you and Peter?"

Sarah laughed. "I'm never rich enough to own a herd of cattle like that. They belong to Cousin Cephas and he pays me pasture rent to let his cattle graze up here in the summer. There is a big haystack behind the barn where they come to eat when they have no more grass. When the cold weather comes and the snow gets deep, he takes them down to his own barn, but he likes to keep them on the mountain as late as he can. But the calves in the barn belong entirely to Peter. The cousin he has lived with gave them to him, one for every year he has been there, because Peter has been a great help. There's many that have started a farm with not even as much as four calves."

The days went by, each full to the brim, each one different from the rest but all of them slipping along in the same channel. There was no more snow for a time, but the frost would lie heavy and white on the grass every morning, and the pasture slopes were brown and yellow everywhere. Since there was no more for the cattle to eat, Cousin Cephas finally drove them all down to his big warm barn, where they would live until the spring came and the pasture was green again. Constance was sorry to see them go and stood looking after the big shouldering herd as they went down the hill. Jock was running and yelping alongside and really being of some help to his wise mother, Martha, who was driving them so carefully and so ably that it seemed that Cousin Cephas and Peter really did not have much to do. Nicodemus, the bull, with his great shoulders and swinging head, went striding along in front of them all.

Constance waved her apron to them as they disappeared around the turn in the lane. Then she hurried inside, for she was helping Sarah slice the apples for drying. There were a hundred things that had to be done before the winter really came. That was why Sarah was always saying they must do this thing—or that—or the other—before the winter came.

Constance thought it had come when she wakened in the night and heard the hard rattle of sleet against the window. It was colder than it had been any time before, and she pulled up an extra quilt and went to sleep again. In the morning, as Sarah gave them their breakfast, she told them how careful they must be, for the whole hillside was a sheet of ice. They had to pick their way down the lane, holding to the bushes and stepping among the stones so that they would not slip. But before they got to the bridge the sun had come out and everything was melting. Winter was not really upon them after all.

Winter was at some of its tricks, however, as she was soon to find out. When school was over, and they came out at three o'clock to climb the hill, they found that a cold wind was blowing and all the puddles were freezing over. Peter said they must hurry to get home before everything was slippery once more. But they were not to go so quickly, for Cousin Cephas, with an anxious face, was waiting on the road near the bridge, to speak to them.

"A boy from the farm below left our barn gate open," he said, "and four of the cows got out. Nicodemus must have followed them, for his halter rope is broken and he is gone. We are looking for them down here, and have got one of the cows back. But will you take a look across the hill, in case Nicodemus has climbed to the pasture? He might have got up there while the sun was out and the ice was melted. But if he has, there'll be trouble getting him down. Such a big beast might break his legs if he slid or fell. And the wind is blowing up colder and colder."

They all searched as they climbed up the hill, the brownies scattering far and wide, but they did not find him. They called as they went, "Nicodemus, Nicodemus," but they found no sign of him. Sarah and Jock came out to join them and they went higher and higher up the hill. All the brownies went home at last except the smallest one, Tim, with the curly red hair, who still trailed behind Sarah and Peter and Connie.

Sarah's voice sounded more and more anxious as she urged them to look here and then there, "There's going to be more sleet, with this north wind. If he's caught somewhere among the bushes—if we don't find him before night comes—"

It was Jock and Tim who discovered him at last and announced the fact by shouting and excited barking.

Poor Nicodemus was in trouble indeed. He had slipped into the little hollow below the rock where they spread the salt, down a slope so steep that he could not possibly climb up again. He was moving back and forth, although there was scarcely room for him to turn;

[29]

he was muttering to himself as bulls do, and his eyes rolled up at them, wild and bloodshot. He had worn himself out trying to struggle up the side of the hollow, which was as smooth as glass. The three above stood staring at him helplessly. What was to be done?

Peter had brought a rope by which to lead him home. The boy stood thinking, the rope dangling from his hand. It was Sarah who suddenly knew what to do. At the edge of the hollow there grew a very old and crooked tree, hanging down over the edge, with its roots firmly thrust into a great rock. "Peter," she said, "put your arm around the tree and I will take your hand and climb down the slope. Then Connie will take my hand and reach as far down as she can. She is smaller and lighter than we are. I think she can just get the rope through the ring in Nicodemus' halter. Then we can help him up between us."

It was plainly the only thing to do. Peter settled himself firmly, holding fast to the tree. Sarah took his hand and scrambled down over the edge of the ravine.

"Now, Constance," she said.

Connie slid down, holding first to one and then to the other. She clung to Sarah's hand and hung far down over the side of the hollow. Yes, she was going to be able to reach Nicodemus. How terribly big he looked there below her, with his great head lifted high to watch her come near. Could she surely reach him? She had thought before that his broad face looked kind. Did she think so now?

III

Mr. Ethan Allen

ANIMALS USUALLY know when people are trying to help them. The big bull, Nicodemus, stopped plunging and struggling as Connie slid down toward him, and stood watching her steadily, his eyes rolling with terror.

"Poor Nicodemus, good Nicodemus," she said, although she was breathless and the words came unsteadily. She was holding tight to Sarah with one hand, and found it awkward to try to slip the rope through the ring of Nicodemus' halter, with only one hand to spare. She tried, slipped, caught herself and tried again. The end of the rope slid through the ring and she scrambled up, holding to Sarah, holding to Peter, catching at the trunk of the tree. Peter pulled up the rope, holding both ends in his hand, so that he had a steady pull on Nicodemus' halter.

They set themselves firmly, Peter with his knee against the tree. "Be ready to pull when I say three," he directed. "One—two—three—"

No tug of war for a school championship was ever pulled more stoutly. Even Tim lent a hand, although most of what he did was to jump up and down. Nicodemus seemed to have waited for the signal, too. At the first tug on his halter he heaved himself up for a terrific effort, his eyes wide, his nostrils blowing out great snorting clouds. His hoofs cut through the ice in one place, failed to crack

[31]

the hard crust in another. But the pull on his halter was just enough to steady him and he came lurching up the hill, slipping, catching himself, slipping again, but at last, with a fearful heaving and snorting, getting himself safely on the level ground. He stood with his head hanging, his great breaths blowing the trampled snow away, and his sides heaving.

They all patted him and comforted him, "Poor fellow, good fellow."

Peter said, "He was almost done for."

Peter led him down the hill finally, with Jock walking beside, to see that the rescue he and Tim had begun so well was safely carried to its end. Then Tim ran away home to tell the other Guyer children what an adventure they had missed.

Connie sat opposite the fire that evening. She was pleasantly tired, and comfortably satisfied with a full day's work, a successful adventure, a good supper and a long peaceful evening. She thought of her mother and father every day, she had thought of them so much that they seemed part of all this that was around her. She had just finished a long letter to them on which she worked every evening, a very pleasant sort of writing lesson. Peter with papers spread out on the table was doing a sum in arithmetic, one that was not in any of the books: "If four calves eat a bushel of grain in two days—they would have to be worth by spring—" He knitted his brows, the problem was a hard one. But whatever Peter did he did with all his might, and he was not only going to calculate how much the calves should be worth by spring, but was going to see that they would actually be worth it. Jock got up from his place on the hearth, because he was too hot, and came over to lie down with a thump beside Connie. He was getting to be a big dog. He loved her, he loved Peter, he seemed to love red-haired Tim almost as much. Connie was thinking of the Guyer children and she was moved to ask a question which had come into her mind a hundred times but which had always been pushed away by something else.

"How can it be," she said to Sarah, "that there are six children at the Guyer house and three of them are eleven years old and two of them are nine? And I asked Tim when his birthday was and he said he didn't know. So I asked Mrs. Guyer—and what do you think, she didn't know either!"

"She couldn't know," Sarah answered, "because she isn't their mother. The biggest girl and Tim are sister and brother, but the others don't even belong to each other. Hereabouts, when children have no homes and no parents, someone takes them in and all the people in the neighborhood help to pay for their living. Cousin Cephas is the selectman who has charge of such things, and he says Mrs. Guyer is the best person in the world to have them. They have come to her house so young they don't remember anything else. But her hands are very full and she can't be expected, really, to keep track of birthdays."

Connie sat thinking for a long time. "Sarah," she proposed at last, "couldn't we give them a birthday party, just pick out one birthday for them all and bake them a cake? Mrs. Guyer has so much to do; and you and I have a lot to do too, but couldn't we find time for that, Sarah?"

"We could indeed," Sarah answered heartily. "Not just at once perhaps. A birthday party is not so nice in the winter as in the spring. How would a day toward the end of April do? That will give us a good long time to be making presents for all six of them. Then when the time comes I will bake a grand cake. I have a pan big enough, but you and Peter will have to help me stir it."

Cold weather had not really come, even yet, and bright autumn days still followed, one after another. While Sarah and Constance were busy in the house hanging up strings of onions and corn to dry, boiling down apple butter and pickling eggs, Peter was toiling even harder than they to get ready for winter. Early every morning and for the short time after school that it was still light, and through all of the long Saturdays, he worked over in the woods, cutting winter fuel. Cousin Cephas, in part exchange for the rent of the pasture, had sent up a man to chop down the trees that had been chosen, and to help Peter saw up the big trunks. Now they must be cut smaller and split, and, since there was a great amount of it, the wood was being exchanged for all the things they needed.

On top of the hill above them lived old Mr. Sam Breen, "a smart farmer" as everyone described him, who had raised on his high acres more corn and hay and apples than he needed, but who did not have any broad stretch of woods in which to cut fuel. He was exchanging with Peter, therefore, and had already brought them onions and apples, pumpkins, corn and hay, for which Peter was to bring him loads of wood as they were ready. He drove rather sharp bargains, Sarah said, but all he gave in exchange was fair and good. Cousin Cephas was also getting wood from Peter and had lent his oxcart and the big pair of black and white oxen to haul it. Peter was to keep them in Sarah's barn until the wood was all cut and carried.

Constance used to bring his lunch to him Saturdays, across the side of the hill to the farthest edge of the farm. Jock would go leaping and jumping ahead of her, and their feet would slip a little on the smooth brown grass, sometimes with the frost on it still, even at high noon. The valley below would look very distant and quiet, half hidden in the faint autumn haze, and the noise of Peter's ax would come very loud to their ears, through the still air.

Connie wondered sometimes if she would really know when winter came, but certainly there was no doubt of it when it actually arrived. Every morning when she opened her eyes she could see the great shoulder of the mountain beyond her window. There had been traces of autumn red in the woods that covered it, when she first came; then it was bare and brown with darker patches where the pine trees grew. And now, one morning, she suddenly awoke to see it smooth and white, with all the roughness of rocks and hollows buried and only the dark shapes of the stretches of pine woods still distinct in the midst of the snow. She sat up and looked and looked. Something within told her that she was not to see it rugged and brown again until spring.

It was exciting to come out into the sharp cold, with the snow squeaking underfoot as she and Peter set off to school. Jock scampered and barked and rolled over on the hard surface, but Peter came tramping along behind them both, looking serious. "The snow is earlier than usual," he said. "It's going to be a long winter. And we haven't got all the wood in yet." It seemed that the first day of winter gave one a great deal to think about. But Connie did not think much further than how beautiful it was.

School had been going on long enough now for them all to be fairly well settled down at their work. Connie found, a good deal to her surprise, that she did not read as well as some of the others, and that her writing was not the best in school either. But in geography she easily led them all. To have a dear father coming home at the end of months of absence to tell her all about the places he had been, to Spain and Portugal, to the ports of North Africa, even on one long voyage that she thought would never end, to China— all that had taught her much. His letters, too, and her mother's, told her about the islands and cities of the West Indies, so that she could tell them all that Santo Domingo and Haiti were on one big island, that there were miles and miles of sugar plantations in Cuba, and that fierce Indians and runaway slaves lived on some of the little islands of the Lesser Antilles. She could even explain about the Trade Wind which was always blowing, and which had given the name to the Windward and the Leeward Islands. She must have known how to make it all very clear, for all the classes stopped studying when Constance Anderson stood up to recite her geography.

She was in the middle of the lesson one morning and was standing in front of the big map pointing to the chief cities of England, when she stopped suddenly; for there was a stranger at the door. Very, very seldom did visitors come to the little school, and this one was unlike anybody she had ever seen before.

He was very tall, taller than anyone she had ever known, and had great broad shoulders and a big chin and twinkling blue eyes. When he stepped over the threshold, he moved stiffly, as though the years had been hard on his joints; but as he came into the room he looked like some great rugged tree, so big he was and so powerful, the kind of tree which has stood against half a hundred storms and will stand against many more. He was bareheaded in spite of the cold, and he wore a leather jacket.

"Go on, little lady," he said to Connie who had stopped in the middle of a word. "Go on. It is good to hear of London as just a

He went straight to the blackboard, and wrote in big letters.

name on a map, not as the place where King George used to sit among his councilors and deal out what he called justice to the rebels in America."

"Indeed, sir, the lesson was just finished," Connie said. She did not feel afraid of him at all, big and strange as he was. His broad smile, which was like a mischievous boy's, would make any person feel at ease.

The man came striding down the aisle between the benches and came up on the little platform where the master's desk stood. "Now bless you, Jonathan Ennis, I've been of a mind, this long time, to visit this school of yours." He went straight to the blackboard, rubbed out all the neat figures which the schoolmaster had set out upon it, took up the chalk and wrote in big letters:

TODAY IS A HOLIDAY

He looked first at the children with a beaming smile and then turned a questioning glance at the schoolmaster to see how he would take it. But Mr. Jonathan Ennis was all smiles also. "There is no one else in the world who could come into my school and declare a holiday, no one but you, Ethan Allen," he said. "You can have your way wherever you go, for every person in Vermont owes you a debt of gratitude."

The big man thrust his great hand through his hair and made it stand out in all directions.

"When I was a boy," he said, "and used to sit in school with my legs too long for the bench and the lesson too hard for my wandering wits, I used to dream of how someone might, just possibly might, come by and step in the door and say to the schoolmaster,

'This is a holiday.' I know you like your school," he finished, turning to the rows of excited faces above the desks, "for you have a good schoolmaster, but no school is ever the worse for a little change and diversion, so I propose that we have it. Since it is near noontime, we will all have our lunch first. Let's see what you have. Can any of you give a wandering stranger a bite of what you have brought?"

They could indeed. Out came all the boxes and bags, with crusty bread and jam, with apple butter, and brown nutty cakes, sections of pie and rounds of maple sugar. The fire was built up and they all gathered in a circle about it. When they were all settled and the flutter of surprise and delight had died down, Mr. Jonathan Ennis made a little speech.

"This, my young friends, is Mr. Ethan Allen, the man who has given Vermont—given her everything she has. He has stood for her rights against those who would have oppressed her on every side. In the war which set America free from England, he has fought with courage. He has been a friend of Washington. He has been a prisoner of war. And I am very proud to say that he has long been a friend of mine, and that he can have anything for which he asks me."

Ethan Allen spoke after him. "I ask no more than that these children should have just such a day as I longed for myself, when the spelling book and the arithmetic became too much for me. Now, my friends, draw up to the fire and set your cheese to toasting and put your apples down to roast. We have everything here which should make a feast for a king, for an even better one than King George. And I have a pocketful of chestnuts to roast among the apples."

It was a feast indeed, bountiful through generous sharing, varied with cookery before the fire which Ethan Allen had learned in soldiers' camps, spiced by such gay talk as kept them all in gales of laughter. When they had finished eating, he began telling them tales of Vermont when it was a young settlement, not yet a state, and claimed by both New York and New Hampshire as part of their domain. Connie had heard from Sarah and Peter about the Green Mountain Boys, the band of young men whose leader was Ethan Allen, how they had defended the rights of Vermont and then, when the war of the Revolution began, had marched away to defend America's freedom. She had come to understand that this great rugged man of the frontier had been more than a soldier, more than a helper and friend to George Washington; that he had been wise in the plans for Vermont's future, that he had advised patience when she would have quarreled with the other states, that he had brought her into union with the other sister colonies at last. She looked at him, sitting there on a stool before the fire, long and lean and weather-beaten, an elderly man but still brave and wise and full of spirits.

The boys gathered around him but the girls had kept a little apart, surprised and wondering and whispering questions among themselves. But Connie crept nearer and nearer to hear what he was saying, to listen to the story that he was pouring out to the boys who hearkened almost without breathing, so afraid were they that they would miss a word.

"It was one of the times that the Green Mountain Boys had not had the best of luck, and they were slipping away into the hills so that the king's men should not catch them. But the redcoats were marching in on every side, and presently we found ourselves between two bands, one coming up the road before us and another marching from the other direction round the curve of the hill. We crept into the covered bridge and lay there in the dark, seven of us, waiting and wondering what would come next. One band of soldiers went into camp and we saw them putting up their tents and kindling their fires. But we could still hear the others coming, tramp, tramp—away off along the road. We knew for certain that by and by they would come across the bridge."

"Was it—was it—our covered bridge?" Connie asked breathlessly.

"That very bridge you cross every day to come to school. We lay there in the dark and we whispered together about what to do. I was leaning back against the wall, and I felt one of the boards give, for some man who worked on building it had been in haste and had not driven the pegs that fastened those boards deep enough. It gave a creak in the quiet and we held our breath wondering if the redcoats would hear, but they did not. And it gave us an idea."

He stopped for a moment to look at the intent faces in the circle around him. Even the girls were, every one, pressing close now, to hear.

"We pushed the board free—gently, oh, so gently—so that it did not make a sound. Then we pried at another, stopping to hold our breath when it creaked, but the soldiers in the camp never heard. When we made an opening, we slipped through it, one after another, and dropped into the stream below. The pool is deep and we made little sound, not much more than a fish jumping. We were crouching on the bank below when we heard the second band of soldiers come across the bridge, tramp, tramp, tramp. One of the riders carried a lantern and we saw it flash through the opening.

[42]

He stopped and looked a little puzzled and said to his comrades that these Yankees were bad builders, look at this great gap they had left in the wall, a man might stumble through it in the dark. Then they joined the others and doubtless all told each other what a rousing fight they would give the Green Mountain Boys—when they found them. Our clothes were wet and so were our guns, so we could only slip away over the mountain and wait for a day of better fortune."

The time had passed very quickly, so that now it was three o'clock and time for school to close. Mr. Ethan Allen got up and buttoned his deerskin jacket. He shook hands with every boy and girl in the school. "I am glad to have had a little talk with you," he said. "Now that all the hard work is done and Vermont is a peaceful state at last, I like to see the young Vermonters and to wonder what they will do. Peter Macomber, I will walk across the bridge with you and Miss Constance, for I am going your way."

They went slowly, Ethan Allen leading his big black horse, so that they could talk as they went along. It seemed that he often made these journeys through Vermont, stopping to talk to all the people he knew. "I was always a restless boy," he said, "and life has not made me any less so. And I know every inch of the Green Mountains from north to south, and I like to pass over them now and again just to find peace in knowing that they are always the same."

He asked them many questions about Sarah Macomber, whom he knew, it seemed, and esteemed highly. "A fine woman and a brave one," he remarked. "And with the pair of you to help her, she will make good this plan of living on her farm again. But it is a struggle the first year; wind and snow, fire and water—how a farmer's heart goes over and over them as the months and years go by; for they can serve him well or they can destroy the good of all his work. Remember that, you two, for it is the whole wisdom of a farmer when he has learned how to meet them."

"Are you a farmer, sir?" Constance asked.

"Bless you, everyone in Vermont is a farmer," he answered. "That is how we all live in a new state, for Vermont is still new and has most of her great affairs before her. And no person has ever come to live here who does not love the land."

He stopped then, for they had crossed the bridge and reached the foot of the lane. "Give my highest respects and regards to Sarah Macomber," he said, "and tell her that I am glad to see that the spirit of adventure is still alive in her heart and those of her two stout helpers. Give her all the aid you can. By spring you will know whether you are winning to success or whether the task has been too hard. I pray it may not be."

They talked fast over the supper that night, telling Sarah all about the day. When they got up Connie was surprised to see Peter putting on his heaviest jacket again and winding his biggest scarf around his neck. "Will you need all that just to go out to the barn to feed the cattle?" she asked.

"I'm going further," he said. "I promised old Mr. Breen that I would bring him his first load of wood tomorrow and he told me to be sure to, for he had very little left. I loaded the cart before I went to school and now it is getting so cold that I am afraid he needs it this very minute. So I am going to yoke up the oxen and take it to him now."

Connie expected Sarah to object; but she was wrong.

"You're right," said Sarah. "Fires mustn't go out when weather

[44]

like this has begun. But you can't go all the way alone, Peter, with no one to walk ahead and carry the lantern. Constance and I will go with you. Run quickly, Constance, to put on your warmest clothes. And set the lamp in the window to light us coming home."

"But won't the stars light us?" Connie exclaimed.

Nevertheless, she lighted the lamp and set it in place. As she wrapped herself in her warm cloak she heard the creak of the wheels, the heavy breathing of the oxen and Peter's voice ordering them to turn to this side or that. Sarah hung the lantern over her arm and stepped out, closing the door behind her.

"It's snowing," Connie exclaimed.

It was, indeed, coming down thickly in the glittering, shiny flakes that sometimes fall in the extreme cold. It lay like diamonds all about them in the light of the lantern. No one seemed to think that this was any reason for not setting out. Sarah took Constance by the hand and went up the lane, with Peter and the big oxen trudging stoutly behind them.

IV

The Frost Garden

THE WAY up the hill might have seemed long, but to go on a night errand through the snow was so unusual that Connie had no idea of its being hard. The oxen walked steadily and evenly and, now and then, as the lantern swung, Connie could see their broad white faces, so serious and so intent on what they were doing that each time she had to go close and give one and then the other a grateful pat. They all climbed up the lane, past the Guyers' house where lights in the upper windows showed that the brownies were going to bed. Connie had not often been further up the hill than that. Old Sam Breen's house was not much of a place to go to, although he had a pleasant-faced, rather shy little wife who hardly spoke above a whisper. She never came down to see Sarah, though Mrs. Guyer often managed to, no matter how busy she was.

The lane became very steep and narrow and finally was not more than a rough track up the bare hillside. The sparkling snow still swirled about them. The way was very steep, so that Connie was out of breath and Jock came to walk beside them instead of galloping on before. Sarah and Peter did not seem to mind. Sarah walked steadily ahead with the lantern, showing the way; the oxen came behind with Peter trudging at the shoulder of the big beast beside him and swinging them this way or that by the sound of his voice.

It was not very late, so that there were still lights in the Breen

The sparkling snow still swirled about them.

house as they came up the last rise of the path. Connie knocked as she and Sarah stood on the doorstep, and Peter guided the oxen in through the barnyard gate to halt the load of wood before the door of the shed. Mr. Breen opened the door, his face all surprise at the arrival of visitors at such an hour in the snow. When Sarah explained why they had come, his wife, who was standing behind, gave a little cry of relief and delight.

"I was worrying so, and the baby has a cold. How very kind of you to come—"

"Hush," Breen ordered her to be silent. "It was no more than right. The boy owes us a load of wood and certainly this is the time when we need it. I won't say it's not a convenience to have it tonight instead of tomorrow, but it's only as it should be that Peter should get it to us. I'll go out and help him unload."

Sarah and Connie sat down by the fire to wait, while Mrs. Breen fluttered here and there, not seeming to know quite what to do with her visitors. She showed Connie the baby asleep in the cradle. "I was so afraid the house would get too cold," she kept repeating. "It's going to be bitter tonight." She drew a long breath and then, as though she had to get up her courage, hesitated and stammered and then said, "Sarah Macomber, you hadn't ought to go out in this snow again. You and the boy and girl should stay the night."

Connie looked about at the bare little house with its two rooms opening off the kitchen, and wondered where there would be beds for them. Probably they would have to sleep on the floor.

But Sarah only smiled and said, "It's not so very bad, and oxen never make any ado about going through snow. We'll get back safely enough, never fear."

Sam Breen came in presently with Peter. He stood before Sarah and spoke very seriously. "I've often been of a mind to tell you, Sarah Macomber, that you're very foolish to try to make out through the winter in a farmhouse alone—a person of your age, with only youngsters to help you. It's hard for a strong man, let alone a woman. You'd best give it up before the cold settles down for good. You never can manage it."

"I think we can," returned Sarah quietly. "I believe Peter here lifted as big logs as you, unloading the wood. He was able to bring the cart up the hill to you; it was he who thought he ought to. And Constance here, she's as neat and quick about helping me as though she had been born to it. And I may not be young, but I can work still. I think we'll get through the winter safely, Sam Breen, though thank you kindly for your thoughts about us."

But this was not all that Sam Breen had to say. He hesitated, but finally went on with determination. "I've supplied you with corn and flour and other things, Sarah, and I was to get my pay for it in wood. But now the winter has shut down so early, I'm not sure I can wait until the boy cuts it. You know it takes a boy a long time, cutting wood outside of school hours, and he not having a man's strength. I think I'll have to ask you, Sarah Macomber, to give me money instead of what we arranged for. It's only fair that I should."

"I suppose so," answered Sarah. Her voice was very low. "But you know very well that I haven't any money to spare just now, Sam, after paying off the debts on the farm."

"That's just what I say," he insisted. "You have no right trying such a thing as this, a woman, two children, and not a cent of real money to pay your way."

"Farmers don't very often have money," Sarah answered. Her

eyes had a hard clear brightness such as Connie had never seen before. "You know all that very well, Sam Breen. Well, we'll do what you want, if you must have money. And now we'll go." She took up the lantern which had been standing by the fire.

Mrs. Breen had carefully put it out and now had lighted it again. "I do believe the oil is a little low, Sarah," she said. "Sam, can't we give her some to make sure it burns until they get back?"

"We've only a very little ourselves," Sam Breen answered, "of course, if they really have to have it——"

"Not if we can't pay for it," Sarah answered with her head held high. "Thank you, Anna, and don't worry. Good night, Sam."

She opened the door and they went out together. The marks of the wheels where they had come up the hill were beginning to disappear as the snow drifted over them. Peter held the lantern now and Sarah walked behind with Constance's hand in hers.

"You could ride in the cart," she said, "but it is better in this cold to keep walking."

They went on, their heads bowed to keep the sharp wind from their faces. Jock still went first, his hair and ears all blown back and his face powdered with snow. Connie knew now why sheep dogs' eyes are all overgrown with hair—it is to keep the snow out on just such nights as this. It was heavy walking now, for the snow was soft and deep, and they plowed and stumbled behind the oxcart. It seemed to Connie that they had gone a long, long way and that the path was growing rougher instead of easier. The light of the lantern seemed to be growing very dim. Suddenly Peter stopped the oxen and turned to speak to Sarah.

"I'm not sure that we're in the track any more. We should have passed the Guyer house by now, but I have not even seen it. And

[51]

the oil in the lantern is giving out. The wind has made it burn faster, and now it is gone."

They stood still, the snow settling on them and beginning to pile up about their feet even as they stopped for a minute. Sarah tried to peer into the dark about them, but there was nothing but white lumps that might be bushes or rocks, and the thick swaying curtain of snow all around. The lantern gave a flicker and went out. Constance almost cried out as she saw the spark dwindle into darkness, but she put her mittened hand before her mouth to keep that cry back. Sarah spoke evenly and calmly.

"I think we have missed the way. We must leave it to the animals, they will know how to get home. Jock, Jock, where are you? Home, boy, home."

Peter dropped back a little and let the oxen take their own way, they swung to the left and moved in a wide curve. Were they just trying to get away from the wind or did they really know? Jock moved with them, yes, it must be that they really were certain of what they were about. Connie could not ask questions or even wonder, she simply stumbled on behind the creaking cart, on and on and on until she thought the way would never end.

Suddenly she felt Sarah's hand close more tightly upon hers. "Connie, do you see anything?"

Constance brushed the snow from the edge of her hood and peered through the dark. "I do. I see a light! It's the lamp you told me to set in the window. And I thought we would never need it because it wasn't really dark when we went up the hill!"

They stumbled over the doorstep and came into the quiet warm kitchen with the fire only just falling into coals, with the ruddy light of the lamp reaching into every corner. Connie thought it was the most beautiful place that she had ever seen. Peter had gone on to the barn to get the oxen safely into their stalls. Connie and Sarah had the fire leaping high, and hot food on the table when he came in. Sarah had taken off her hood and shawl and was bustling about, stirring the pot, putting plates on the table. Connie sat on the bench by the fire and looked at them both. Her knees were trembling; she was tired out; she had been frightened. What a terrible mile that last one had been! She expected every moment for one or the other to begin, "Wasn't it dreadful—" But neither of them did.

"Well," thought Connie, "if they can take it so quietly, I can too." And she said no word, not even when she got up obediently as the clock struck her bedtime. But Sarah held her very close as she kissed her good night, and came into her room later to tuck her into bed, with a big jug of hot water to keep her warm, and an extra feather quilt to cover her.

"It's going to be chilly," was all Sarah said, however.

When she was gone, Connie could hear the branches of the trees crackling outside, in the stillness of bitter, terrible cold. The sky had cleared; the snow would be all diamonds again in the starlight, Connie thought, with her face buried in the pillow. Should she sit up and try to see? No, she was far too sleepy.

In the morning she could see nothing through the white panes of her window, so thickly had the frost pictures covered them. She missed the sight of her great shoulder of the hill and the clear morning sky above it, but she would see it soon enough again, she was sure.

When she came downstairs, she asked Sarah, "How soon will the white melt off my window so that I can look out at the mountain again?"

[53]

"Oh, maybe in three months, or four," Sarah answered easily. "Now and then it might be clear for a day or two, but it will really be covered with frost pictures until the spring comes."

As they worked together that morning Sarah seemed very quiet and did not hum the little song that they usually heard when she was washing the dishes. She had a pleasant way of doing the dishes and the cleaning and such things herself, and letting Connie have the more exciting tasks of stirring the Indian pudding and skimming the cream. Connie had learned to carry a big milkpan across the kitchen without spilling, and that is more of a feat than anyone knows who has not tried it. A wide milk pan will slop over, just as a saucer will, if it is not held exactly steady.

Even Peter noticed that things were not as they should be, and stole more than one glance at his grandmother, as he went in and out. But he said nothing to her, only whistled a little more cheerfully than usual. Peter was a very good whistler.

But when they sat at the table at noon, and Connie and Peter, both looking up together, saw that Sarah was scarcely eating and caught the glint of tears in her eyes, Peter asked bluntly, "What is the matter, grandmother? I know something is."

Sarah's face quivered a little, but she spoke steadily. "I have been thinking all day of what Sam Breen said. And I wonder if I do have a right to risk staying on here through what is plainly going to be a long winter. I wonder if it is not going to be too hard on you. I'm not young, he's quite right. And you are not very old. And I—I haven't any money."

They could have contradicted the first of the things she had said, but to the last there seemed no answer to make. Sarah had no money. And Sam Breen was insisting that she pay him some. Peter knitted his brows as he thought about it, but Connie could only stare help-lessly. It was Sarah herself who finally found the thing to say.

"I believe I am tired, and that is why I am letting myself worry. People should never decide anything important when they are tired. If we should have to give up living here, we won't do it without thinking it over very thoroughly. For I think if we give it up, Peter and I, we would probably never come back to the farm. Now I am going upstairs to rest, for there isn't much to do this afternoon. Constance can lie down to sleep or she can sit here in the armchair in the sun and read to herself. No one is to work any more today."

They both went upstairs with her. Usually Sarah did not allow herself the luxury of a fire in her bedroom, but she did not object now when Peter brought in wood and kindled a cheerful blaze. Connie covered her with the gay quilt, and Sarah gave her a quick, bright smile before she shut her eyes.

It was very queer to see Sarah resting in the daytime; but, after all, she was right in saying that people should not decide things when they are tired. Connie and Peter went down again to the kitchen, saying nothing, but each thinking deeply. What went through Connie's mind was the pressing question: If Sarah and Peter had to give up the farm, where would she go? She had felt so safe and settled and happy there, surely there was not to be another change! She looked about the bright room, with the sun making a checkerboard on the scrubbed floor and knew all of a sudden how much she loved it. And if it was already dear to her, what did it mean to Sarah and Peter?

What Peter was thinking could only be guessed, but with Peter, thinking meant doing something at once. Before Connie knew what he was about he was getting down his woolen scarf and his big coat.

[55]

"If I go somewhere, Connie," he said, "can you get along alone? I might not be back until late tonight, or maybe even not for a day or two. Do you think you can keep up the fires and feed the calves? I will bring in some more wood from the barn, the wood closet is nearly empty."

"Yes, surely I could," Connie said. She was delighted to think that there was anything she could do to be of help. "If you are going anywhere, you haven't very much time. Don't stop to carry in the wood, I will do it."

"You're right, I don't have much time and I have quite a long way to go," Peter answered. He did not tell her what he was going to do, although he must have known that she was burning to know. He hesitated a minute, in fact, as though he were about to explain, and then shut his lips firmly. "I don't know if it will come to anything," he said finally, "and if it doesn't, I don't want anyone to be disappointed but myself. I'll tell you all about it when I come home."

He went out, with a breath of clean, cold air blowing in as he closed the door. Jock, suddenly waking to find that something was happening, rushed to the door and begged to go out. Connie thought a minute. It would be a long afternoon and she wanted Jock with her. But Peter would have a lonely walk, wherever he was going. She opened the door and Jock went racing away over the snow. She caught a glimpse of Peter; he was coming out of the barn and leading the biggest black and white calf. His face was very sober. Just what could he be planning to do? She watched him go down the hill, the calf pulling back now and then, as calves love to do, Peter humoring him and persuading him. Jock snuffed at his heels, to urge him forward. The dog was growing very wise about driving

[56]

cattle; his mother Martha had been teaching him. Connie wondered what in the world Peter was planning to do with the calf, but she had no real idea. It was very pleasant and quiet in the kitchen. The fire was still burning brightly, she need not fetch the wood yet.

She sat in the big chair, with a square little old book which she had got down from the shelf. It had small print and queer little pictures, a book of English ballads, exciting stories in verse. Connie was presently absorbed in it. She had been so busy that it was some time since she had found any spare moments for reading. She would just get to the end of one thrilling account of knights and ladies, perhaps then just begin another one. . . . The sun moved across the floor, Connie read on, the kitchen began to get dark. How hungry she was for a story, after all the busy hours that had kept her from reading. She loved especially the tales of Robin Hood and of his adventures in Sherwood Forest. They reminded her a very little of the stories she had heard of Ethan Allen and his good companions, the Green Mountain Boys. She went straight through the book, and closed it with a snap after she had finished the last page.

The kitchen was surprisingly dark—and very cold. How could she have let so much time pass! She jumped up and ran to the fire, the logs had dropped into ashes, there were only a few coals left. She must put wood on quickly—but there was no wood. She had forgotten to bring it in. And it was time to feed the calves!

The first thing she thought of was to run upstairs and ask Sarah what to do. But Sarah was so tired she must not wake her unless it was absolutely necessary. Sarah's fire would have gone out long ago, of that she was sure, for Sarah had only let Peter put on a stick or two—"just to take the chill off the room." And if the kitchen fire went entirely out, how would she light it again? She would have to go up to the Guyers' perhaps, to get coals to carry back. And it was snowing once more, snowing hard. Oh, how cruel winter was!

She looked at the fire again. If she ran to the shed for more fuel, would it have gone out altogether when she got back? She must risk it and certainly she must hurry. She threw her cloak around her and dashed away toward the barn.

Many Vermont houses are built with the woodshed at the back of the house and the barn at the back of the kitchen and woodshed, and the pigsties at the back of the barn, so that the whole thing looks like a telescope drawn out joint by joint. But Sarah Macomber had preferred a sunny kitchen with air on all sides, so that the shed was not built next to it. Connie had to run across a broad stretch of snow to reach the low shed door.

It was bitingly cold, so cold that her breath positively froze in her nostrils, but she ran so fast that she could not think of anything except that the snow was hard and smooth and that she must not waste any time by slipping. She picked up all the wood she could carry, chips for kindling, thin white birch logs, a whole armful—she could come back for the bigger ones. Her feet fairly twinkled as she sped back to the house. She was breathless as she knelt down before the fire.

How clumsy her hands seemed as she heaped up the chips and laid the logs over them. Surely they would catch at once. She would go back for the bigger logs. She went out to the shed again, knowing more and more fully what a stormy night it was going to be. She came back into the kitchen and saw the fireplace still dark and cold; her fire had not caught at all. She knelt down before it and peered in through the wood. There was a faint, a very faint glow of coals still; the fire was not entirely dead. She felt in the woodbox for one last piece of the dry birch bark which always caught so quickly. There was a little piece hardly bigger than her hand. She laid it next to the coals, took up the bellows and began to blow, oh, so carefully, lest she blow out what little fire there was. She held her own breath. Suppose that last flicker of red should disappear into dead gray coals? Was it glowing a little redder, was the fire really living instead of dying? She fed it one chip and then another, still holding her breath in anxiety, for fear it would not catch.

She looked about at the dim room, at the blank windows behind which was that bitter cold which was bound to come in if she could not fight it back. And suddenly she cried out within herself, almost aloud, "I hate it. I hate the cold. Why is it always trying to get at us?" Yes, she hated it, but she was not going to be beaten by it, nor was Sarah. Sam Breen had said that Sarah did not have enough help to struggle against the winter. She would show Sam Breen and everyone else that she could be a help, a real one. She glanced back at the fire. A little flicker had crept across the surface of the log, then, suddenly, the smooth white bark had caught and burst into flame. Another log was ablaze, and then another; the fire was really burning—it was crackling and leaping up the chimney, driving back the shadows, driving back the cold. She got up from where she had been kneeling so long on the brick hearth that her knees were stiff. That did not matter. She had fought the cold and beaten it.

Now she must go out and feed the cattle in the barn. She knew just how to do it, she had held the lantern many times and watched Peter. And she would bring in more wood when she came back.

The big door of the barn slid back easily and she stepped inside. It was warmer there, for the breath of the cattle and the warmth of their big bodies took off the edge of the cold. But how patient they were to stand so quietly in their stalls in the darkness. She could hear the oxen pulling at the hay, and the calves stamping, restless and curious as to who it was who had come in. In the light of the lantern their dark eyes shone out at her as she went from stall to stall.

She gave them corn, she brought them water, she climbed the ladder and threw down hay from above. Sarah would not let her use a pitchfork, but she could throw the hay in armfuls down into the stalls. When she opened the door into the corn crib, two little field mice with stumpy tails went scuttling past her feet. She was not frightened, she knew field mice moved into the barn and expected to live there through the winter, just as surely as the cattle did. She fed the oxen first, then the calves, then moved on to the hen house that connected with the barn and scattered corn for them. They took it with grateful cluckings and chucklings, rather soft and sleepy in the dark. When she came back through the barn, the oxen had finished eating and with grunts and lurches were preparing to lie down. She always liked to see them do it, to watch them drop their heads, kneel, then lower their great hindquarters and settle down on the straw with a last grunt of satisfaction.

"Good night," she said to them all, as she went out and closed the door.

Even before she came into the house she saw the dancing firelight through the window and thought how warm and safe it all was within. She hoped Sarah would not be awake, so that she could begin to get supper ready. No, everything was still quiet upstairs, so she put the kettle on, laid the table and began to stir up batter cakes with a practiced hand. How much she had learned since that first night when she had felt so proud of finding a bowl of bread and milk for Jock. She missed Jock but she was glad that Peter had him.

When everything was ready, except to make the tea and put the griddle for the batter cakes on the fire, she sat down to wait until Sarah should wake. She sat down in Sarah's chair by her own little table, where the glass lamp always burned for her sewing. There was a book or two beside the sewing basket, the top one was the Bible. How often Constance had seen Sarah sit down, tired after a full day and open her Bible to read a little before she took up her evening work. Connie felt a good deal like Sarah now; she thought she would go on doing just as Sarah did. She took up the book, and the page that spread before her was one that Sarah had so often turned to that the book opened of itself, close to the beginning.

Connie read slowly, "While the earth remaineth, seed time and harvest, and cold and heat, and summer and winter, and day and night shall not cease."

Yes, that was how it was, and people had known it from the beginning of time, summer and winter, heat and cold, you must learn to meet them all, as surely as you saw night follow day.

She sat there a long time thinking of the stately words. Then she got up and went to the window, forgetting that she could not look out, because of the thick white frost on the pane. She stood looking at it and cried out suddenly, "Why, it's a garden."

A garden it surely was, with feathery ferns, spreading trees and little paths leading up and down. There was even a tiny crisscross fence across one corner. No two panes were alike, but all were covered with the strange white flowers. She was still examining it when Sarah came downstairs, very different from the tired, anxious Sarah who had gone up to rest.

"I can't think when I have slept through a whole afternoon like this. But how rested I feel now!"

[61]

She looked about the bright kitchen, at the crackling fire, at the singing kettle, and the neatly laid table. "I was wondering," she said slowly, "whether I ought to go on with living here, I wondered and wondered until I went to sleep. But when I have such help as this, when you can do all this work and sit there looking gay and happy over it, why then I believe I need not be so anxious after all. We will talk it over with Peter, and then we will decide."

Connie closed her book and got up to set the batter cakes to cooking. She explained to Sarah that Peter had gone on an errand and had taken Jock and the calf. She pressed her face against the window, yet she could see nothing at all but the darkness and the snow coming down. Where had Peter gone, she wondered, and when would he come back, and what news would he bring?

V

The Barn Raising

PETER WALKED down the road with the calf following at the end of his rope and with Jock walking quietly beside him. They were all three very serious, for this, indeed, was a grave matter. Peter did not really have any complete plan; he only felt sure that the way to repay Sam Breen was to turn the calf into money and, since it was a good calf, that ought not to be impossible. He knew, however, that it would not be easy, for in the middle of the winter people would not be buying. He remembered that Mr. Ethan Allen had said that he would be spending the night at Cousin Cephas' house, and Peter thought that the two men between them could give him some advice about what to do.

His face was very sober as he went plodding along, for he loved the sturdy little black and white animal which came after him, most of the time so willingly. But he had thought, more than once, as he added and divided and multiplied that long arithmetic sum which he went over so often—if four calves eat a bushel of corn in two days, how much will they eat in five months—he had thought that it might turn out better to get rid of one calf, and that, if he did, this one should go. He had made up his mind firmly, so that now he would spend no time in feeling badly about it. But it is a large matter to go about selling a calf, when you have never done it before. He would need plenty of advice.

[63]

He was just crossing the bridge when he heard the sound of horses' hoofs behind him, hollow and echoing even with the snow on the ground. He looked about and saw the big black horse and the tall bony figure which he knew instantly belonged to Ethan Allen. The man drew up alongside him and asked in his gay, breezy voice, "Whither away, man? This is a strange sort of time and weather for taking calves to market."

Peter laughed delightedly. All his doubts and solemn feelings were gone. He knew at once that Mr. Ethan Allen would help him. Without any hesitation he began to tell him all about their affairs, and about how his grandmother was worried over what she owed to Sam Breen.

"Do you think a calf would cover it?" He asked anxiously when he had finished.

Ethan Allen looked at the calf carefully. "If you sell the beast— well, it would cover it all and give something over. Now the thing is to see about who wants a calf and who can pay you for it. The two don't always go together. If you feel like traveling along with me, we will surely find somebody."

They went steadily along the snowy road, past Cousin Cephas' house, for Mr. Allen said he had an errand first, and moved on down toward the valley, the snow hard under their feet, the trees loaded with white. They talked busily. Peter learned that there were some important matters concerning the State of Vermont to be settled at the next elections, and that Ethan Allen was journeying up and down the country urging the people to make no mistakes in their votes.

"Farming people live so far apart," he explained, "that they do not always find out the real truth about such matters."

[64]

They were all three very serious, for this, indeed, was a serious matter.

Peter knew that all through the most troubled time of Vermont's history, it was Ethan Allen who was leader and adviser and who counseled his fellow men well. He was a very brave soldier also, but it was his wise leadership, more than his bold courage as a fighter, which had helped Vermont. Mr. Allen seemed to know every man, woman and child in his state and, as the two went along and passed one farm after another, he had something interesting to tell of the family which lived in every house. Sometimes he got down and led the calf and made Peter ride, but his gay flow of talk never ceased.

They had reached a corner where a little lane branched off the main highway, when Ethan Allen drew up his horse.

"I want to ride up and see how Jenny McGowan is doing," he said. "I hate to ask you and this black and white friend of yours to travel two miles out of the way, but I cannot go by this place. Jenny has four fatherless children and, at the very best of it, they are as poor as poverty itself. I am always anxious about her."

They turned aside and made their way up the rutty track toward the little gray house that stood at the end of it. They had hardly come halfway before they saw someone coming toward them, a tall boy, a few years older than Peter, very thin, and with his hands in the pockets of his ragged jacket.

"Hello, Dick McGowan," said Ethan Allen, stopping his horse. But the tall lad only gave him a queer look and hurried past on the other side of the road. Mr. Allen looked after him, and called his name again; but the boy did not even look around, only hurried his long strides down the hill.

"Now, that's a strange way for a friendly boy to act," Ethan Allen said. "I've known him since he was hardly more than a baby and never has he had anything but a cheerful word for me before."

[67]

He urged his horse on, and hurried up the hill, with Peter following, and the calf, tired now and hanging back on its rope, trailing behind. They came to the door, where Ethan Allen got down and knocked, and went in at once.

The bare room inside was cold, with only a little fire struggling on the hearth. A baby was crying in its cradle drawn up close to the fire, and a woman was sitting rocking it, swinging it back and forth with her foot on the rocker, while she knitted a long gray stocking and gave directions to her oldest daughter, who was about Peter's age and was washing the dishes. Through the window Peter could see a little huddle of sheds which were all the farm buildings, although some tall posts and a framework of boards showed that someone had undertaken to build a fine big barn, but had never got beyond a beginning.

"What's wrong with Dick?" Ethan Allen began bluntly at once.

"Dick, oh, Dick's gone away from us," Jenny McGowan answered. She hardly looked around at them and her voice was dull and tired. "He's been talking for a year of how he wanted to go to be a sailor, and I always told him he couldn't leave us, being the only one big enough to help with the farm. But today he just said all of a sudden that he could not bear this kind of living another minute and off he went."

"But what will you do without him?" Ethan Allen demanded, looking around at the dreary room and the dying fire.

Peter thought of his grandmother's bright warm kitchen and wondered how two places could seem so different.

"I don't know myself what we will do," Jenny McGowan answered.

Ethan Allen went to the window. "That's a fine big barn your husband began to build," he said. "You must need it badly, with your cattle all huddled into three little sheds."

"Yes, and Dick tried to work on it, after his father was gone, but what can a boy do alone? With everything in such little space the work is twice as hard as it should be, and I expect Dick just lost heart. I told him again and again how wrong it was to leave us, but a day just came when he couldn't think of anything except how he wanted to be away. But I must give you some supper, sir, you and the young gentleman. What am I doing sitting here and lamenting, and you probably hungry as hawks after your journey? And did you say you had a calf with you? Go out to the barn and give him whatever you can find; there's plenty of straw at least to give him a warm bed. You must sleep here tonight; for it is getting dark, and too cold to travel further."

She got up and began bustling about the kitchen. Ethan Allen went with Peter, although not to help him put the calf to bed. He began talking eagerly the moment the door had closed behind them.

"Something has to be done for her," he declared. "I thought there was something strange in the face of Dick McGowan, when we met him coming down the hill. Going off to be a sailor was he, and leaving his mother and the rest of the family so badly off they hardly even have food to eat? But he's a good boy. I think things were so bad he just didn't know what to do."

He walked to the barn, deep in thought, while Peter went beside him, wondering what anyone could do when things had gone so very wrong. The sheds were crowded with cattle, horses and pigs, all huddled under the narrow roof. He found a corner for the calf, gave him a bed of deep straw and climbed up to the loft to throw him down some hay. Even while he was fumbling about in the dark, he heard Ethan Allen call joyfully from below, "I have it, I know what to do for them. I vow it will work."

When Peter came down he was surprised to see Mr. Allen saddling his horse again. "You are to sleep here tonight," he directed, "but early tomorrow you are to set off on the north road and tell them at every house that the next day there is to be a barn raising, at Widow McGowan's. I will go on the south road with the same message, and it may be I can overtake Dick and talk a little reason into him. But what the boy needs, what they all need, is a helping hand."

Peter could hardly believe it when he saw him galloping away down the hill. He stood looking after him, his mind full of anxious wonder. He thought of his grandmother, brave Sarah Macomber, and wondered if things ever could possibly come to such a bad way with her. It is a hard thing for a woman who tries to manage a farm, and who has the long Vermont winter to face. Here at the McGowans' there was so little grain in the corn crib, so little hay in the loft, so many crowding around the fire there in the bare house. Would Sarah Macomber ever be threatened with such want as this? No, he promised himself, never, never, while he had strength in his arms, and courage in his heart. What—what could Dick McGowan be thinking of to go away and leave such a task undone?

He went back to the house to find a hot supper set upon the table. He explained that Mr. Allen had suddenly decided to attend to some business on the south road, and would not be able to stay there tonight. But he, Peter, would be glad to, and to leave his calf for a bit, if he might, since Mr. Allen wanted him to do an errand for him in the morning.

Peter was hungry enough for two, and the poor little supper was scarcely more than enough for one. He slept on the bed they made

[70]

up for him beside the fire, and was up very early next morning. He saw that his calf was comfortable in the stable, and set out with Jock along the road on Ethan Allen's errand. He gave his message first to a man who was passing on horseback and got his promise that he would come to the barn raising.

"Jenny McGowan is in bad luck, is she?" the man said. "Surely, I'll come to help her, and bring something along. I'll tell everyone I see."

Since he was riding in the direction of Cousin Cephas' house, Peter asked him to leave the message there and also to stop at the school and get word to Connie "that I can't get home today or tomorrow, but that I'm with Mr. Ethan Allen and everything is all right."

He spent the whole day tramping the cold roads, carrying Mr. Allen's message as far as he could go. Everyone he saw promised to tell others, everyone was kind and interested and promised to come. He was warmed and fed as he went along, and sometimes given a lift down the road, but he walked many cold miles just the same.

"This isn't selling my calf," he said to himself now and then. What was he to do about selling the calf? He asked several farmers for advice but not many could offer much.

"It seems to me Silas Simmons was on the lookout for a likely calf," one man said. "But everyone knows Silas drives pretty close bargains."

His wife, who was stirring the pot before the fire, turned round as she heard his words. "Silas isn't the only one that wants a calf. Didn't I hear Ebenezer Hillton ask you where he could get a good one?"

"Why yes," her husband answered. "But there's more hope from Silas than from him. Those two are the smartest traders in Vermont, and could bargain a goat out of his horns and tail. Once in my life I saw one trying to buy a horse from the other. It was a rare sight, I can tell you, but neither could get the better of the other one and they gave it up. But I'll see that they come to the barn raising. It's surely time we all did something for Jenny."

Peter tramped back to the McGowan house that night, cold and tired and doubtful over what he had been doing. He could not tell so very many people, one boy, walking the snowy roads through the whole of a bitterly cold day. And he had been away from the farm on the hill, from his grandmother and from Connie, much longer than he had intended, and not one inch nearer had he come to selling the calf. When he got to the dreary little house up the lane, and found that Ethan Allen had not come back, his heart sank heavily. What could ever really come out of this sudden plan? But still he could not go on without trying to offer a helping hand to Jenny Mc-Gowan and her children. He managed to say nothing of the barn raising and went to bed early among his blankets before the fire.

A barn raising or a house raising is a gathering of all the able men around to help some one person to build his barn or his house. It is not only the men who come, but the women and the bigger children too. The men bring their tools, and lumber if it seems to be needed; the women bring big baskets of food, cakes and pies and pickles and hams, for the dinner in the middle of the long busy day. They bring their sewing and their knitting and often their babies, and spend the day together while the men toil outside. With so many to work, the barn goes up as though by magic, and the man for whom it was built lends his own aid when some one of the others needs help. Peter had never happened to go to one.

The next morning was bright and cold, with the snow as smooth and hard as marble. Even while they were all eating breakfast they heard the sound of sleighbells and saw a big man drive into the yard with his rosy wife and two tall daughters all crowded on the seat beside him. He was driving a farm wagon set on runners instead of wheels, and had piled it high with boards and tools, with two big sacks of corn on the top. When his wife climbed down, he handed her the basket with the legs of a plump yellow chicken, new bread and a beautifully scalloped pumpkin pie showing under the cover which would not shut. A little sleigh came jingling into the gate directly behind him, this time with a single stout man and a great bag of apples. Others followed, more and more men and women usually with their children with them, all talking, laughing and joking, glad to see one another as a change from the long cold days when each family was busy in its own house. It was like Christmas, Peter thought, as he saw them coming in, bringing their helpful gifts, each person able to offer only a little, but all of them together piling up a happy abundance on the table in the middle of the kitchen.

The McGowan children shouted with delight as each new family came bustling in, stamping the snow off their boots, their cheeks glowing with cold and excited pleasure.

"You shouldn't do it, you shouldn't ever do such things for me," Mrs. McGowan kept saying as the pile of good things grew and as Peter and the smaller boys began carrying sacks of grain away to the barn.

One man had brought a whole load of hay, "I had a good season, Jenny," he explained carelessly, "and even my greedy critters couldn't begin to eat the barn empty by spring." He and Peter tossed it into the loft, where there had been so little before. Another had a load of wood.

Cousin Cephas was there, so busy working that he had only time for a nod and a smile at Peter. A man came in soon after him whom Pete had never seen before. He was tall and big-shouldered, but with a narrow face. Peter heard Cousin Cephas speak to him.

"Well, Silas Simmons, how are things up your way?" Peter stared at him earnestly. Did he look as though he wanted a calf? This seemed hardly the time to ask him.

When a good crowd had gathered, the men went to work at the barn. Such hammering as there was, and such sawing, such shouting of orders, and all lifting together to get a big beam into place. Peter had never believed that work could go forward as quickly as this did. Even the boys helped. Peter carried orders, brought nails and buckets of hot coffee; he bore his part when ten men together lifted on a big timber.

He began to glance about to find Ebenezer Hillton, who was also said to be looking for a likely calf. Someone pointed him out at last, a very little man, sawing awkwardly at a big beam.

Presently they all came trooping in for the gigantic dinner, with half a dozen pots bubbling before the fire. Then they went to work again, since darkness would come early, "and we're bound we're going to begin roofing before we have to stop," as the tall man vowed who was giving the orders. It was true that they actually had finished the sides of the barn and were beginning on the shingles of the roof when it grew so dark that no man could see any longer to hammer a nail. As they came in, Peter heard them arranging among themselves, "If you can give a day's work, Dan, I'll give another,

[74]

and begin where you left off." It was plain that the barn would be covered in and ready for use within a week or two, if the weather held clear, and with every man in the neighborhood ready to turn his hand to finishing it.

It was a most cheerful company that sat down to supper. Peter, sitting rather quietly in his corner, was glad to hear the talk and laughter, but it would have been oh, so much gayer still, he thought, if Mr. Ethan Allen had been there. How he wished that he would come in, how he wondered why he did not. The big jolly man who was taking charge of things, Joe Hallowell, was cracking jokes and setting the company into roars of laughter, but somehow it was not as though Ethan Allen were at the head of the table to lead them all.

Jenny McGowan's kitchen was not big enough to hold the whole company, for some extra helpers had come in the afternoon. The supper table was set in what was called the summer kitchen, a place at the back of the house and much like a shed. There was a fireplace in the big chimney there and in it had been built up such a tremendous blaze as had not often roared up the chimney throat. Here was room for the long tables and the abundant supper and the people going back and forth with steaming plates and bowls. Oh, if only Ethan Allen would come in to sit at the head of the board, Peter was thinking. He caught a glimpse of Jenny McGowan's face as she went hurrying past. It was wreathed in smiles one minute and then suddenly clouded and downcast. She too was thinking of someone who should be there, her oldest son, who had tramped away in the cold and the snow, too heavy hearted to go on with the struggle that was before them all. She stopped a minute beside Peter, and spoke to him as the one person who would understand.

"If he had known we were to have help like this, he would never have gone away. It was trying so hard and never succeeding that was what made him lose heart. God take care of him wherever he is." She seemed certain that Peter knew of whom she was thinking. He did.

The men had finished eating and had pushed back their chairs and were talking easily. Peter could see Silas Simmons, halfway down the nearest table, finishing his third slice of pie, without hurrying. He had said little during supper but plowed steadily through one heaped-up plate after another. At the other table Ebenezer Hillton, an active, nervous man, was talking and laughing and jerking his hands about as he told a long story to his nearest neighbor.

"I wish Connie could see all this," Peter thought suddenly. How far away Sarah and Connie seemed, in the quiet house on the mountainside, sitting down to their supper and wondering where he had gone and what he was doing. He had done nothing to carry out his real errand, so far, but he could not have done otherwise than help Mrs. McGowan so far as he could. The others had done so much, and all he had managed was to walk a few miles up and down the road. Ethan Allen had said, "We are bound to do anything we can for Jenny McGowan." Yes, he, Peter, had done what he could, but it was not much.

The voice of one of the men near him grew louder and broke into his thoughts. "We've done the best we knew, but I wish there was something more. It seems to me I never did see a family get so deep into trouble as these McGowans, and it's not their fault. It's not even the boy's fault that he went off. If we'd helped a little sooner it would have given him courage to hold out. But we just didn't know how hard things were. They're not easy for anyone."

Another man spoke. "What we have left for them here won't

take them through the winter. They ought to have something more. But I can't think of anything else we can do just now."

He might have said more, but there was an interruption. The room had got very hot with the big fire and someone had opened the outer door a crack to let in some of the fresh, cold outside air. There was a little push at the door, now, and it swung open, letting in a new guest to join the gathering, an inquisitive guest who had felt lonely out in the barn and come to look for his master. It was Peter's calf.

It stood on the threshold, peering timidly in, its wide ears spread forward, its big, surprised, wistful eyes turning questioningly from one person to another. A calf is a pretty animal; this one of Peter's, clean limbed, smooth coated, half bold, half timid, was a real beauty. Every man there was fitted to understand that this was an unusually fine one. A little silence fell as they all studied it, and as it raised its square little head and sniffed.

One man said in a slow drawl, "There, Silas Simmons, ain't that just the sort of calf you were telling me you wanted?"

It was not Silas Simmons but little Ebenezer Hillton who spoke up in reply. "It's a likely enough critter. Dunno but as I might think about buying it, if Jenny McGowan was of a mind to sell it, and don't want too much."

Peter had opened his mouth to tell him, no, the calf was not the McGowans', when something stopped him. Was it a tap on the window pane close beside him? He thought he had been mistaken, but then he heard it again, tap, tap, tap, tap. He pressed his face close to the glass, for it was hard to see, from the bright room inside, out into the darkness. But he made out a tall figure against the white of the snow. One? No, two. A face came close to the glass from within; it was Ethan Allen's. He was beckoning to Peter.

[77]

There was such a close crowd around the outer door of the shed, looking at the calf, that he slipped through the main kitchen and out the front way. Yes, sure enough, standing in the shadow of the chimney was Ethan Allen with someone beside him, a long, shambling boy with a drooping head. It was Dick McGowan whom they had seen yesterday, tramping down the hill to run away to sea.

Ethan Allen laid his arm on Peter's shoulder and drew him aside.

"I found the boy after following him a long way," he said in a low voice, "and I got him to turn back. But now he's here he won't come in. And, indeed, he vows he's going off again anyway. I'm not going to lay strong hands on him—whichever he does has to be his own choice. I've said all I can, but a man can't understand everything or know what is the right word to offer. Walk down the hill with him, Peter, and if you can, find the thing to say that will keep him here."

Suddenly, as he was speaking, big Dick McGowan swung about, broke into a run and dashed away down the hill. Peter, with all the strength of a pair of stout legs, set out at full speed after him.

VI

Striking a Bargain

ALTHOUGH PETER was running breathlessly down the steep lane, he still, somehow, had time to think or, it might be said, a few thoughts were jolting about in his mind as he stumbled over the frozen ruts. Never, he was sure, had a harder task been laid upon his shoulders than this one which Mr. Ethan Allen had given him. Mr. Allen could persuade anybody to do anything, so people said, and if he had failed what could Peter do? Nothing, so it seemed. Yet he vowed inside himself that he would bring Dick back, somehow, no matter what he had to do. But he did not really know how in the world it was to be done.

The older boy's long legs covered the ground easily, for he knew his way and Peter did not. But even when he was falling behind, Peter stumbled obstinately on, feeling his breath coming short, stubbing the toes of his cold feet on the hard clods in the lane. Dick would have got completely away from him except that his knowledge of the ground gave him too much confidence, he took a long stride on uncertain footing, slipped and fell full length. By the time he had got to his feet, Peter had caught up with him. He stood there under a big bare maple tree, and faced Peter.

The snow was coming down, a light feathery snow that fell without a sound. Peter tried to catch at his gasping breath, tried to think of something to say, and could not. It seemed that since Dick had

[79]

found he could not shake him off, he had stopped to have things out, and was waiting, with all the cold, still white world about him waiting too, for what Peter might have to say. And still Peter could not speak.

In the end it was Dick who spoke first. "Well," he said impatiently at last. "Did you think you were going to take me by the collar and lead me back? Because you can't."

"No," Peter agreed. "I know I can't." Dick was at least sixteen years old, to Peter's twelve, with all the difference in size that anyone would expect. "But I have to make a try, somehow," he finished frankly. "Mr. Allen said I surely must bring you back."

"I suppose you think I'm a brute, going away from them all like this," Dick went on. He seemed to have made up his mind now to make Peter understand, before he went on his way. "Maybe I am a brute, but I can't go on at home like this any more. It's—" his voice shook a little, "it's all so hopeless. One day like another, one year like another and never anything better. I don't mind the hard work, what I mind is never having anything of my own and always working on and on just the same."

"You never have anything of your very own?" Peter exclaimed. "Not a horse, or a dog, or a cow?"

"Nothing—ever. How I've wanted a horse, a good horse, not the broken-down scrubs we always have to get because we have no money. Yes, I know the neighbors have helped, but that doesn't make it really seem any better to me. I've worked and hoped and waited, always thinking I could get somewhere and never doing it. So now I'm going to leave it behind me, no matter what anyone thinks."

He turned away and strode off along the lane, not running this time, but walking steadily as though he were quite certain that Peter understood now how determined he was and would not follow. He came to the bottom of the lane and swung into the main road. If Peter could not stop him, he was truly on his journey.

A terrible resolve had grown up within Peter. He had made up his mind that at any price he would do what Mr. Ethan Allen wanted. The cost was dreadful, but he had weighed it carefully, even in that moment of standing there. His grandmother was badly off but here was someone in much greater need. A lump rose in his throat, so big a one that it almost choked him, but he ran after Dick and caught him by the arm.

"If you will stay," he said, speaking a little huskily, because of the lump, "if you will stay, I—I will give you my calf. Two men up there are talking about buying it already. If one of them does, the money for it would be a start for buying a colt, and a colt would be a horse by and by. You said—" he concluded awkwardly, for Dick was standing still in the road now staring at him, "that a horse was what you wanted. Well, this would be a chance for a horse—"

He was talking on, trying to fill up the queer silence, when Dick at last interrupted him.

"You would do that for me," he said, "all that, just to have me go back?"

"I would," said Peter. Nothing would turn him from his purpose now.

Dick stood quiet, thinking deeply. "I didn't want to listen to what Mr. Allen said," he admitted reluctantly, "but if you would do a thing like that, why that makes the whole thing look different. You really mean you would do it?" It seemed impossible for him to believe.

"Yes," Peter stood his ground, "I really will do it. And you'd better hurry back because they may have the calf sold before you get there."

So it happened that twenty minutes later, two very cold and snowy boys, walking side by side now, and talking like the oldest of friends, threw open the door of Jenny McGowan's kitchen. They found her alone there, sitting by the fire, wiping her eyes on the end of the gray stocking she had been trying to knit, a stocking for Dick even though he had gone away from her. Jock was lying beside her feet on the warm bricks of the hearth. Beyond, in the summer kitchen, a great hubbub of voices was going up. The children were all in there and Mr. Ethan Allen's voice could be heard above all the rest. But Jenny McGowan had slipped back to sit alone and mourn over the one who was not there, her son who had gone way from her—forever.

"Mother," Dick cried.

She looked up, the tears still wet on her face.

Peter walked on into the other room. In the summer kitchen everyone had gathered in a big circle, and at the center of it stood two men—and the black and white calf. Because the outer kitchen was so nearly like a shed, the calf had been allowed to stay there.

The two men were Silas Simmons and Ebenezer Hillton. Each, it seemed, had made up his mind to buy the calf and was driving his bargain against the other. Ethan Allen, sitting in the biggest chair beside the table, was seeing that there was fair play and was urging them on.

"It's one of the best calves that ever came under my eye," he was saying as Peter came in. "I would have bought it myself, in a minute, only everyone knows I haven't any money. A man can't have adventures and lay up a fortune, all in the same lifetime. But a clever

They found her alone there sitting by the fire, wiping her eyes.

man like you, Eben Hillton, oughtn't let a fine beast like that slip through his fingers."

Ebenezer Hillton looked desperately about him. "I never gave more than four dollars for a calf in my life," he declared, "and here you've somehow got me into offering six. I don't know what's taken hold of me."

"I'll offer seven," Silas Simmons returned promptly. There was a gasp of astonishment in the crowd, as there is at a riding exhibition when a horse takes a higher jump than has ever been achieved before. In that time, calves sometimes sold for half a dollar. Peter's calf was a good one, well grown and well fed. But only one man's determination that the other should not get it was making a price like this.

"Seven dollars," Ethan Allen repeated. "Now, Eben, it's your turn again. Are you going to see that calf grow up in Silas' barnyard and tell yourself every day that you might have had it for your own. Come on now, eight?"

"Eight dollars." The offer came from Ebenezer Hillton in something like a groan, while a roar of applause went up from the men who were listening. Every one of them was a born trader, as Vermonters are apt to be. Peter was a good one himself, so was Cousin Cephas. Ethan Allen probably was not, for it was well known that he had gathered no riches, but he knew how to make the most of any such quality in other people.

Silas Simmons was the sort of man who would make a good bargain, the sort which leaves both sides satisfied, but Eben Hillton would take what he could and give as little as possible. The men were old rivals, each was always trying to outdo the other, but not for years had they come together in just such a contest as this. They hesitated, blustered, grew more and more excited as people do when they are playing at a game. This was their game, and it carried them beyond their usual caution. Silas would offer more than Eben, Eben would choke, grow red, hesitate and then offer more than Silas. The price rose and rose, beyond anything that had ever been paid for a calf in Hebron township, so that the men who were looking on stared at one another in astonished delight. They slapped their knees and cried, "Go it, Silas. Go it, Eben. Don't let t'other do you out of it."

Eben Hillton spoke at last, in voice thick with strong feeling. "That's my last offer," he said, "and may Silas choke on it." Ethan Allen stood up and held up his hand. "If you can better it, Silas," he said, "we'll call this deal closed." There was a breathless silence.

"I'll better it," Silas said quietly. His face was red too, and his eyes were dancing.

"I'll—I'll—" Eben began to stammer, but Ethan Allen interrupted him firmly. "You said it was your last offer. And we'll call the deal ended. It's a sinful price for a calf, yet it was worth it to us to watch such a trade. But I won't stand by and see two men force each other higher. Come on, Peter Macomber, and turn over your calf to him."

"Peter Macomber?" repeated Silas in astonishment. "Isn't the calf Jenny McGowan's?"

Peter was standing by the door. Everyone turned to look at him as Ethan Allen addressed him, and in the surprised silence he had to lift his voice thin, and alone. "It's not mine, it's Dick's."

Ethan Allen shot him a quick look. In that second each understood everything that the other would have said.

"Dick's, yes, Dick McGowan's," Mr. Allen repeated. "Well,

Peter was, you might say, the cause of the sale, so he shall have the real price of the calf and Dick McGowan shall have the rest. That's justice, and no man shall dispute it." No one ever disputed Ethan Allen. It was not worth while.

Now it was time at last for the company to scatter. The men harnessed the horses; the women bundled themselves up; there were many good-bys and last messages shouted as the sleighs went jingling out of the dooryard. Jenny McGowan, with her eldest son beside her, said good-by, offered thanks for such great kindness but, when they were all gone, turned suddenly to her tall boy.

"Don't," he said before she could speak, "don't ask me why I did it."

She only shook her head. "I'll never ask you. I'll never think of anything but that you came home again."

Ethan Allen made a sign to Peter. It was time for them to go also. Jenny McGowan might have tried to keep them, might have made some effort to speak of gratitude, but she had no chance to do so. They slipped out of the back door and crossed the snowy ground to the stable. Cousin Cephas was still there and so was Silas Simmons. While the backs of both men were turned, Peter put his arms around the neck of the calf to say good-by to it.

"Don't you mind," said Ethan Allen. "Silas will be kind to the calf and it will grow up to a good life on his farm. That's why I stopped the sale just when I did, for I didn't want Ebenezer to have it. Eben's not kind to his creatures and he's a trifle too stingy with his grain."

Cousin Cephas was to take Peter home with him in his sleigh. Mr. Ethan Allen had saddled his tall horse and was leading it out.

"I'll see you soon again, Peter. We've had a pleasant bit of a jour-

[87]

ney together. Some day we may set out and travel farther. I'm always going somewhere and I like you for a traveling companion. Maybe we'll do great things together some day. Vermont always needs someone to work for her future."

He swung into the saddle and went galloping away. Peter stood looking after him, until Cousin Cephas said gently, "It's time to go, Peter, and you're going to see him again."

As they jingled homeward, tucked under the warm blankets, with Jock galloping ahead, Cousin Cephas told Peter tale after tale of Ethan Allen, how he had come to Vermont as a young man looking for adventures, and how he had become leader of the Green Mountain Boys who had worked so bravely to keep their state from being wrecked by the greedy and dishonest men who wanted to get possession of her lands, how he had fought in the war of the Revolution and captured the Fort at Ticonderoga with only a handful of men, how he had been taken prisoner at Quebec and had suffered in an English prison and come home at last with a still unbroken spirit.

"He was a wild lad," Cousin Cephas said slowly, "and I don't doubt it was in his heart a hundred times to run away from home just as Dick McGowan would have done. And he might have led a wild life of wasting all his days if he had not found a great work to his hand, setting up a new state. He put his whole soul into that and forgot everything else. Boldness and love of adventure can serve a man and his fellow men well if they turn in the right direction. We all love him. The time is passing and he is no longer a young man. May he be spared to us for many years to come."

Cousin Cephas did not drive in at his own gate, but crossed the bridge and went on up the hill with Peter beside him. "I'm going to see that your affair with Sam Breen is carried out as it should be," he said. "You have a little more money there than you really need for paying him, but he will try to say you owe it all. Make him promise you a lamb when he has one in the spring. He will be willing to do that. Then you will have changed your calf for a sheep and paid your grandmother's debt into the bargain. That won't be a bad trade."

Connie and Sarah were sitting quietly by the fire, wondering, in Sarah's words, and for the hundredth time, "where Peter could have got to." Suddenly the door was burst open and Peter, cold cheeked and rosy, excited, and full of news, came running in. "Oh, grandmother, I've seen Mr. Ethan Allen, I talked to him, Silas Simmons has my calf, we don't owe Sam Breen anything any more and he's going to give me a Cheviot lamb."

"There now," said Sarah, "what in the world is the boy trying to tell me? Did you give your calf away, Peter? And what is all this of Mr. Ethan Allen? There's never any knowing in the world what that man will do next, but it's bound to be for something good, though he takes his own way of doing it. Now sit down and eat your supper. It's way past your bedtime this very minute."

But Connie's comment came more slowly and was very solemn. "We're going to stay on the farm now. Peter's got us past the hard part, and it's going to be easy now."

Sarah's face was very bright as she stirred the fire. "There's plenty left that's going to be hard," she remarked, "when one thing seems to end, another is just about ready to begin. We won't know whether we are going to be able to last through the winter, until we have done it." But her voice sounded very cheerful as she added, "Anyway we will keep on trying."

[89]

VII

The Sugar House

As THE days went by and turned into weeks and then, almost as quickly, so it seemed, into months, Connie began to find that she was learning a great many things. It was not just that her reading and writing were getting better, although indeed they were improving fast. It teaches little girls a great deal just to write a part of a long letter every night to dear people who are seeing wonderful sights in strange lands and who want, for that very reason, to hear all about every single little thing at home. And to get interesting fat letters in return, written in a square plain hand that is so easy to make out, to run through pages that tell of ships and palm trees and coral islands and flying fish, that teaches anyone to read. Peter was almost as excited as she was over the arrival of the weekly letter. "Read that aloud again about the pirate ship that chased them south of the Virgin Islands," he would beg, and Connie would go over it again. Captain Anderson's ship was one of the swiftest in the New England ports and had little to fear from pirates. But it made them both tingle with excitement to read about the chase. When the coach stopped running, a man on horseback would carry the mail up from Hebron Village and leave Connie's letters either at the schoolhouse or at Cousin Cephas' farm. Everyone was interested in them and it made Connie feel very important to have them all stand listening as she read aloud snatches of the news the letters contained.

No, it was not just in school things that she was learning so much. Nor was it just that she knew how to knead bread now, and mix biscuits and churn butter. She was good at understanding directions and at remembering them afterwards, but she had always had a way of spending a great deal of time over the things which she liked, more time than was reasonable. But at last she was getting over that and coming to see how one thing must follow another at the proper time if the day's work was to be done.

She said in surprise to Sarah one day, "You don't have to keep telling me to go on with this thing or that thing any more. I'm beginning to see how I have to finish one thing in time to do another, so that everything fits together in a pattern."

Sarah nodded, well pleased. "That means you are learning how to work," she told Connie with approval. "You learn how to work as you learn how to read, and one is almost as important as the other."

It was not all work, however. There was time now, since Connie learned to get things done, to read in the afternoon after coming home from school, to sit by the fire with three round red apples and a book and follow a tale or a ballad until it was the hour to begin supper. At other times she and Peter and the brownies would get out their sleds and go skimming down the slope of the hill, guiding themselves carefully around the rocks and turns and gliding smoothly, slower and slower, out into a level pasture before they came to a stop. They played games in the snow and made snow men and caves, they built forts and stormed them with snowballs. Eight children of all ages and kinds can find a great deal to play at. One of the best games was building islands out of snow, and making voyages from one to another, from Cuba across to Jamaica, fleeing from pirates off the Bahamas, and rescuing shipwrecked mariners who had gone

[91]

aground on the dry Tortugas. They all knew to the minute when they must stop and Peter must go to tend his precious calves, the brownies must run to carry in the wood for Mrs. Guyer, and Connie must set to work to make applesauce and batter pudding for supper.

There was skating, too, on the deep pool of Hebron Brook. And more than once Cousin Cephas took Connie in his sleigh on a swift jingling drive down toward the village, with the snow flying like spray from under the horses' feet and their big hindquarters all dark and rough and furry as she looked up at them from her low seat among the thick robes. Cousin Cephas' brown colt looked almost black, with its winter coat all thick and standing out against the cold.

"I believe I like cooking as much as sliding," Connie announced one day as she was stirring the stew in the big pot. She felt very important as she swung the iron crane off the fire, just as the stew got to the right bubbling heat and must not cook too fast.

Christmas passed and New Year's. Snow was added to snow, with the first still unmelted but buried deeply by what had fallen later. A smooth, curving white drift had built itself up before one of the windows, on which the wind had carved swirling curves and patterns that looked like the ripples on water. The frost garden was thick and white still on the upper windows, but the warmth of the kitchen melted those below so that Connie could look out, could even open one of them at times to let in a wonderful breath of cold fresh air.

And one day, when many weeks of winter had gone by, she opened the window on a cold sunny morning and saw a little bird swinging among the twigs of the bare grapevine, a lively gray bird with a black top to his head which gave him the look of having pulled a dark cap down over his eyes. Connie had seen him before, but never had she heard him sound just that little song, high and clear, two notes together, one after the other.

"Listen," said Sarah, stopping her busy broom that she might hear better, "that's the sugar bird."

"I think I have heard my mother call it something else," Constance said.

"Oh, yes," Sarah agreed. "Its real name is the chickadee and you always know him by his chickadeeing so cheerfully in all the coldest weather. But my grandmother used to tell me to listen for him, that when he sounded that new little spring song it was time to make maple sugar. That was why her people always called him the sugar bird."

All winter Connie had heard about how maple sugar was made, and now she was to see it. Cousin Cephas came up to help; he and Peter drove about in the maple-tree grove which Cousin Cephas called the sugar bush, and put little pegs and chips into slits in the bark; then, when the sap of the tree began to run out along them, they put buckets below to catch the clear white liquid. Later the oxen came, pulling a big heavy sled with great barrels on it, and into these the maple sap was emptied to be boiled down over a crackling fire in the snow, until it was sweet thick sirup. Cousin Cephas took a share of it for his part of the work, the rest Sarah put away in jugs to be boiled again and made into maple sugar when she needed it. Connie loved to help, to bring wood and to stir and taste and to bank snow around the big kettles to hasten the cooling.

It was on one of the last days that they were working that Sam Breen came across the hill and asked them for the help of the oxen since he had got his sledge with a heavy load of barrels frozen into the snow, so that his horse could not pull it.

[93]

"It's not far away, just below my sugar house," he said.

Connie walked beside Cousin Cephas to where the sled was stuck in a little valley among the trees. On the slope above stood the small square building where Sam boiled down his maple sap. Cousin Cephas began unhooking the horse's traces and made ready to hitch the oxen to the loaded sled.

"Have you got any lambs yet, Sam?" he asked. "I hope you're counting on giving Peter a good one, the kind he bargained for."

"We bargained for a Cheviot," said Sam Breen, " and that is what he will have. I'm a man of my word, when once it is given."

Cousin Cephas chuckled. "Yes, I do know you will keep it, Sam. But see that you keep it in full. Steady there," he said to the oxen, "now pull away."

The heavy sledge slid away behind the oxen as easily as though it weighed nothing. "We'll just draw it across the ravine for you," Cousin Cephas said. "Your horse is a willing beast, but he's tired out."

The sledge went slowly over the hill into the little valley, down which ran the brook which was now buried deep in ice and snow. There was a narrow road beside it, which Sam Breen used to haul wood. The little track made a turn and crossed a log bridge. Cousin Cephas stopped the oxen and stood looking down at the course of the stream.

"As soon as it thaws, you ought to shovel out that bed of gravel, Sam," he observed. "It's piled up so that it shows even through the snow. If there's much water in the stream after all this snow melts, it will block things up and make you trouble. This valley is gravel and if the stream runs over its banks it may wash a lot of this hill-side away."

"Oh, I'm not worrying about that," Sam answered easily. "I only haul gravel out of here when I sell it. It looks too much like working for nothing to come up here and dig without any return."

"To leave it where it is might prove to be costly," Cousin Cephas answered, but he said no more.

They followed the track down toward Sam's house, and passed a little orchard which he had set out in the shelter of the valley. With its stout young trees growing in neat rows and squares it looked like the regular pattern of a patchwork quilt. Beyond the orchard the track crossed a ridge and came out on the smooth slope of Sam's meadows. There was a long low shed just under the shoulder of the ridge.

"I keep my sheep up here, away from the cattle," Sam said. "It's a good stout barn, I just put it up last year."

Cousin Cephas halted the oxen and unhooked the trace chains. "I guess the horse can get you home now," he said, and he and the oxen, with Connie and Peter following, went back to their own task. "That shed will be full of young lambs presently," Cousin Cephas told them as they walked along. "I am going to see that Peter has as good a one as Sam promised him."

"Where will all the snow go?" Constance used to ask now and then as she saw how deep it was piled against the fences, walls and tree trunks.

"It will all have to go downhill some time," Sarah, Peter or Cousin Cephas told her. "You'll see the brooks all running full and more, presently, when it once begins to melt." Connie could not help feeling that it never would melt, so long had it lain there, with the bright cold sun having no effect on it at all.

But it was only a few days later that she woke one morning to a strange sound, the patter of drops outside her window, and saw that it was indeed melting on the eaves and that a bright row of drops was trimming the outside of her window frame like a string of beads. The frost garden had vanished in the night, since now the season for other sorts of ferns and flowers was really coming. Connie could hardly believe it, but when she opened the kitchen door to go out to feed the hens, she felt the soft south wind which was blowing up from the valley and warming everything. The snow sounded hollow and brittle under her feet and the surface was soft. It was really melting.

For three days the weather was warm with the snow thawing everywhere. It was in the middle of the morning of the third day that one of the Guyer children came in with a message for Peter. "My father says that Sam Breen has plenty of lambs now and that you had better go up and pick out the one that is to be yours. A man has been up there arranging to buy most of the others, when they get big enough." Everyone, it seemed, was interested in Peter's bargain with Sam Breen.

"I'll go this afternoon," Peter agreed.

Sarah added, "I think Connie and I may as well go up the hill with you, but we won't go to Sam Breen's. I want to go through the sugar orchard once more to make sure we didn't leave any buckets or such things there. But Connie must put on her big boots."

It was a beautiful walk up the hill, with the air warm and clear all about them, very different from that night when they had struggled up the slope with Sam Breen's firewood. Connie ran and skipped and sang. She splashed through the puddles in her heavy boots. Big clouds were sailing over the mountaintops just high enough to clear the summits.

"We may be going to have a rain," Peter said. "It isn't nearly cold enough to snow."

Peter went with them all the way to the sugar bush, saying he could stop at the Breen farm on the way home. They walked through the leafless woods, found a forgotten bucket and some of the iron hooks on which the kettles had been hung. He and Connie scurried this way and that, looking at rabbit tracks, chasing Jock who was chasing squirrels. Sarah walked more slowly behind them, enjoying it as much as they. Almost before they knew it, they had climbed to the very top of the maple grove and could look across to Sam Breen's land and to the place where the oxen had pulled free his loaded sledge. A great cloud had spread itself over the whole sky now and the sun was hidden.

"We will go down this way and see Sam Breen," Sarah said. "But we must hurry. We will hardly get there before the rain begins."

They were crossing the slope, with Peter and Jock some distance ahead, when Connie stopped suddenly. "I hear something," she said. "I don't know what it is." She listened for a whole minute, but the sound was not repeated. Then just as she and Sarah were going on, it came again, tiny but still not so very far away, "Ba-a-a."

Sarah hearkened too. "How could a sheep have got up here?" she wondered. "It must be a lost lamb. Run ahead and call Peter to come back." Connie raced across the slope down the hill into the little valley, then suddenly stopped herself so quickly that she slipped and rolled over and over in the snow. She had almost trodden on something small and white and woolly, curled up under a bush. It tried to get up and gave voice to another faint frightened little "Ba-a-a."

Connie knelt down and gathered it up in her arms. It was a tiny lamb, not more than two or three days old, with smooth short wool, and black feet and a black nose. It gave her one pitiful look out of its big eyes, then closed them. Sarah came up behind. She tried to help Constance carry it, but the little creature struggled so that she had to leave it to Connie. For some reason the lamb was not afraid of her. It lay still with its head buried against her breast, but it was an armful, small and young as it was. She walked forward uncertainly, feeling for a steady footing as she went down the hill. At just that minute Peter and Jock came racing back.

"It's going to rain. There's Sam Breen's sugar house here at the edge of the grove. Get into that. What—what have you got there? Why, it's a lamb!" Connie stumbled on with her burden, Peter helping her the best he could, Jock jumping up in curiosity to see what in the world she was carrying. They got under the shelter of the low roof of the sugar house just as the rain began to come down heavily.

There was no storm or wind, just a flood of rain that came upon them as though the whole cloud overhead had suddenly turned to water. The sugar house was not the best of shelter, the roof leaked and the water came through in streams to trickle over the dirt floor. They had to move about to keep dry. Connie laid the lamb down in the safest spot, where some leaves had blown in upon the floor and made something like a bed. It lay perfectly still, and now did not even open its eyes. Jock sniffed it anxiously, Peter knelt down to look at it, while Sarah stooped above them.

"It is a Cheviot lamb, a very good one," she said. "It must have strayed away from Sam Breen's flock. Cheviots are hill-country sheep and like to climb from the time they are babies. Sometimes when the mother has twins she gets confused about it and thinks that

For some reason the lamb was not afraid of her.

one isn't hers. It takes a little trouble to teach her better. Sam Breen must have overlooked this one. We ought to get it in where it will be warm and dry. Dear me, how long is this rain going to last?"

There was no sign at all that the rain would ever stop. What would have been a soft, steady snowstorm was not coming down in the same kind of rain, dropping straight and quiet with no hurry or no bluster; it was a thorough, diligent downpour, determined never to stop. But it was washing the snow away, so that even as they sat and waited, they saw the bare spots of ground grow bigger and whole slopes of hillside cleared of the drifts which had lain on them so long.

They waited a very long time, thinking every moment that the rain would cease but seeing it grow steadily heavier. Connie took up the little shivering creature and held it close to try to get it warm. When her arms grew stiff, Sarah took it and then Peter. Once in a while its eyes would open and it would give a comfortable little bleat as though it knew that all they could do for it was being done. But they could do very little.

At last Sarah went to the door of the little building and looked out. "I do not see any sign that it is going to stop," she said anxiously, "and look, the stream below is flowing over its banks. I really believe that we should go on, rain or no rain. I don't want to wait here until it gets dark."

"But the lamb," Connie wailed. "If we carry it out through the rain it will get wet and cold, even worse than before. It will be dead before we get it to the house. And if we leave it, surely it will die. Oh, Sarah, don't say we have to leave it." Her voice broke on a sob, she could not think of the trusting little thing being left to bleat and cry all alone. Nor, it seemed, could Sarah.

"It may be that we ought to go," Sarah said, "but after all it might be as bad to go as to stay. No, Connie, we won't leave the lamb or risk carrying it through the rain. We will wait a little longer."

They settled down again, to wait, but Peter was restless. He went to the door and back again, he tried to put his head out of the little window, then went once more to stand on the threshold. Connie and Sarah were so busy tending the lamb that they did not pay much attention to him. But suddenly they both jumped, for Peter had cried out in a strange, startled voice,

"Grandmother, Connie, look!"

There was no time to look. A terrible sound arose outside, a grinding and crashing, followed by the noise of sliding stones. The walls of the little building trembled. Connie, still clutching the lamb tight, buried her head in Sarah's lap. Jock shivered and pressed close against her. "What is it?" Connie cried, her voice muffled against Sarah's knee.

Sarah did not answer; there was a long wait and then, of a sudden, another crashing roar and another long rattling slide of stones and gravel. Jock whimpered aloud and tried to burrow his head under Sarah's cloak. He was a brave dog; but this was more than he could understand or face. Connie cried out,

"Is the mountain falling down?"

Peter's voice came back cheerfully. "Only a piece of it," he said. He was at the door taking observations. "The brook is washing the hill away, and carrying the gravel through Sam Breen's orchard and down into his meadow." He was silent a minute watching and then suddenly exclaimed, "I do believe Sam's sheep shed is right in the way of it. I'll have to go tell him."

He was out and off like an arrow, with Jock racing after him. The rain was still falling as heavily as ever, so that it was hard to see them after they got some distance from the house. Sarah stood on the threshold to watch.

"Oh," cried Connie, "it will come again, the hill will slide down with them."

"They went over the top of the ridge," Sarah answered firmly. "And Jock would never step on ground that was unsteady underfoot. He will find the safe way." Her voice was drowned by another crash, while the boards and timbers of the little house shivered and creaked. But the moment there was quiet she spoke steadily and surely. "I know they got safely over the hill."

"But—but," stammered Connie, "it was so dangerous. How could you let them go?"

It was not a reproach, it was just a wondering question.

"Why," returned Sarah, surprised, "of course I let him go. Sam Breen is a neighbor and he needs help."

VIII

The Feather Bed

THE RAIN, driving in Peter's face, almost blinded him, but still he made astonishing speed across the hill. The footing was bad, with some ice and snow left, even after all the downpour, with stretches of slippery mud and with jutting rocks coming up through the earth and half hidden by the bushes and brambles. But when one is in a desperate hurry, even the obstacles can make for greater speed, with long slides down a slope of ice and snow, with great jumps over the stones, with risk of a hundred tumbles but with such need for going quickly that accidents, somehow, could not be allowed to happen. He was tempted to take a short way, down along the brook, but Sarah's voice, calling behind, warned him. He was hardly over the top of the hill when he heard the deafening crash of stones and gravel below him and knew that the hill was sliding again. The noise rose to thunder in his ears as he came hurtling down the slope, but he did not stop to look back or to listen. He knew what he must do.

Sam Breen had heard the crash of the first slide and had come running up the hill to look to his sheep. Peter saw him at the big sliding doors of the barn, struggling with the wooden latch. He was a slow old man, pale and breathless now as Peter came panting up beside him. But he managed to explain what had to be done.

"We have to slide the doors wide open the minute they pull apart.

If it's only a narrow opening the sheep will trample each other to death trying to get out. Now you take that side, it's jammed and I can't seem to move it. If you can't, we're done."

Peter took his stand, and braced himself.

"Now," ordered Sam Breen and they both pushed at once. The wide doors rolled back.

There came out a river, a torrent of panic-driven sheep. They neither looked nor heeded, they merely rushed after their leader, the big ram who came charging out first. He almost upset Sam Breen who had jumped aside as quickly as any man could. Peter had been a little quicker, but a wildly baaing old mother sheep blundered into him just the same, almost taking him off his legs. The frantic creatures lowered their heads and went galloping away across the field, Sam Breen calling frantically after them.

"There's fifty new lambs," he said to Peter. "It will destroy them all if they get wet through in this cold rain."

Fortunately, the young mothers and the lambs had been at the back of the barn and came out last, or all the little creatures would have been knocked down and run over by the bigger sheep. They came running out with their feeble, frantic little gallop, crying pitifully when they were separated from their mothers in the hurrying crowd. In an instant they had scattered in every direction. Sheep have no courage, they are patient, faithful, uncomplaining creatures, but any reasonable bravery has been left out of their make-up. The big rams will attack an enemy, but when once thoroughly frightened even they do just what all the others do, gallop away with their flock at their heels, until they fall down with exhaustion.

"We'll lose them all," Sam Breen cried despairingly. But he and Peter both stood rooted to the ground, for a strange and terrible

[105]

thing was happening to the sheep shed. They moved back and back to watch in safety. The first of the landslide had come down into the mouth of the little valley, the second had poured its stones and gravel to the very back wall of the long building. Now came the shattering roar again, and another great fall of stones and mud and earth came rolling down, to plunge against the walls and over the low roof. Beams cracked, walls buckled, the roof sagged and fell in, the whole thing smashed together like a paper toy. Peter stood staring simply, not able to believe his eyes, but was recalled to his senses by Sam Breen's sharp order.

"Get after the sheep. They're worth more than the shed."

Jock was the only one who had been giving his whole attention to the real need of that desperate moment. He did not know a great deal about his work yet, but he had all the spirit in the world. He paid no attention to the terrible thing happening above, but raced away after the sheep. He ran, he barked, he stood before the charge of a furious ram, he nuzzled little lost bleating lambs, he turned one back and another, a dozen, but what could one dog do with a hundred terror-stricken animals? The raindrops glistened on his thick gray coat, his round red tongue hung out, his great sturdy legs never faltered in their swing as he ran and ran and ran.

The rain was not so steady now, and the clouds were breaking overhead; the crashes of falling gravel were coming further and further apart, and were not so heavy. The part of the hillside which could slide had nearly all slipped away. But the sheep shed lay buried almost out of sight, and the sheep were still flying all over the hill.

Peter's clothes were so wet they stuck to him like skin, his hair was plastered to his head, he shook his head, as Jock did, to get the raindrops out of his eyes. He went back and forth across the field trying to quiet the sheep, trying to get the lambs together, trying to drive the mothers toward the big cattle barn down near the house. He hardly saw the two figures that came down to him through the rain, and he jumped as he heard Sarah's voice.

"Peter, did you come in time? Are all the sheep safe?"

Sam Breen, who was passing close to him, in pursuit of his youngest ram, answered for him. "Yes, if you can call sheep safe that are running wild in such a rain, lambs and all. But the shed's broken and buried past ever using again. And we'll never get the lambs in before they're soaked and chilled to their death."

Sarah turned abruptly to Connie. "Give me the lamb to carry. Run down the hill to the Guyers' and get them all, every one of the children to come up. It's numbers we need here. Two or three of us can never do anything."

Connie ran as she was told. She was tired, wet, bewildered, but she had enough spirit and energy left to do what she could. It was not far down the hill to the Guyer house. Mr. Guyer was away, he had gone down to speak to Cousin Cephas on business. But the children came running out, all six of them. Even the littlest knew something about driving sheep.

"I'll get on my shawl and run down to fetch my husband," Mrs. Guyer said. "That would be more help than if I come myself. Dear, dear, but I hope Sam gets through this without losing half his flock."

If it had not been for the brownies, Sam Breen might have been ruined forever, as a farmer, all in that one terrible hour. Most of his wealth was in that flock of sheep. If he lost them, he lost nearly everything. And Sarah was right, it was numbers that were needed, a dozen more nimble legs, six lusty voices to shout and drive the frightened animals back in the proper direction, six pairs of arms to

[107]

pick up exhausted lambs and set them beside their mothers; all these accomplished what a man and a boy and a dog had been absolutely unable to do without help. The lambs were collected very quickly, but it was a long time before the last fleeing animal was got into the cattle barn, and Sam counted them all over, seventy-nine, eighty-nine, ninety-nine, a hundred. Yes, they were all here. The lambs were rubbed dry and wrapped in straw. They were sorted out and brought to their mothers, who were unreasonably particular, Connie thought, about insisting that they have their very own children again.

Meanwhile, in the Breens' kitchen, Sarah was nursing the woolly baby they had found on the hill. It was far colder and wetter than any of the others, its eyes were shut and it seemed scarcely to be breathing. Sarah seemed to know exactly what to do, she plunged it into a pail of warm water to get it heated through, then rubbed it dry and wrapped it in a blanket. She put warm milk in a bottle and held up its head to let a few drops fall into its mouth. It was so weak that it could hardly swallow, but little by little the milk went down. Then there was nothing to do but watch and wait. Connie sat down beside her and smoothed the little thing's head now and again with a light hand. It seemed to her that a long time passed before she heard a knock at the outer door and looked up to see three men come in, James Guyer and Cousin Cephas—yes, she had expected them, but who was it behind them? It was Mr. Ethan Allen.

Connie went out to the barn to tell Sam Breen and Peter to come in. Everything had quieted down, the sheep had settled in their new sleeping place and Peter had been helping Sam feed his cows. They were milking now, so that through the dim light of the barn Connie could see the row of stalls, hear the cows munching their

[108]

hay and hear also that odd, comfortable sound that is like no other in the world, the quick sharp spurt of milk into the milking pail. Peter had tried to teach her, but she was not very good. When Sam Breen got up to go hurrying in, she sat down in his place and tried to finish. The smooth cream-colored cow turned to look at her curiously and a little anxiously. She did not make any objections, but Connie felt sure that the cow knew, as well as she herself, that she was not very skilled at milking yet. Peter had to finish for her, finally, but she helped him carry in the foaming pails.

All three of the men were gathered about Sarah and the lamb beside the fire. Sarah was filling another bottle of milk to try feeding it again.

"It's a Cheviot lamb, a good one," Cousin Cephas said. "How did you ever come to let it stray, Sam?"

"Oh, it was like it sometimes happens, the mother had two and one got off among the other sheep and she didn't know it as hers again. Yes, it's a good lamb. It's the one I meant Peter to have."

They were all silent, watching. The lamb struggled a little as Sarah lifted its head.

"I'll hold it," Peter said.

He took it on his lap, while Sarah gave him the bottle of milk. Peter held it to the little thing's mouth. It choked a second, then blinked, then gulped one big swallow after another. It was stronger; it was better—it was going to live.

Cousin Cephas said firmly to Sam Breen, "You could hardly intend that lamb for Peter now, when it's so nearly dead. You'll have to give him another. It would be only just to let him choose for himself, the best one you have. Peter has done a good deal for you this day."

"Yes," agreed Sam unwillingly. "Yes, I suppose he has. Well, if that's the justice of it, he'd better choose him one that satisfies him. Perhaps he's had his eye on one already."

"Well, Peter," said Cousin Cephas, "how about it?"

Peter looked up. The lamb had finished drinking. Connie held out her arms for it. Peter gave it to her. The little creature nuzzled her hand, then nestled down in her arms and closed its eyes with a long breath of content. Peter answered Cousin Cephas' question.

"That's my lamb," he said.

"Why, man, you hardly even know yet whether it's going to live or die," Cousin Cephas exclaimed. "You'd better take one that hasn't been through so much."

Peter looked from Sarah to Connie and then shook his head in firm determination.

"That's my lamb," he said again. "We—we've got fond of it, already, taking care of it and carrying it home. We'll keep it."

Cousin Cephas looked troubled, Sam Breen looked relieved, but Ethan Allen laughed aloud.

"Peter Macomber," he said, "I thought you were a born trader. But now I'm afraid you have much too soft a heart."

Peter looked across at him and grinned. Yes, that was true, but was his heart any softer than Ethan Allen's? There was not much choice between them. He spoke the truth, for he would not have them misunderstand.

"We've got fond of it. But then, besides, I think it is going to be a good lamb. I'm going to risk its not growing up."

Cousin Cephas and Ethan Allen looked at each other and chuckled.

"You needn't be discouraged with him, Cephas," Mr. Allen said.

"He'll be a good trader after all. He has the courage to stick to what he thinks is a good bargain."

It was half an hour later that they all went down the hill. Ethan Allen and Cousin Cephas were to eat supper at Sarah's house, and Ethan Allen was to spend the night there. He was going to set out on one of his journeys early the next morning. Sarah was in a tremendous flutter over having such a great man for a guest. It was the first time Connie had ever seen her when she was not perfectly calm.

"Will you go into the best bedroom and build a fire, Peter? And, Constance, will you put all the bedding before it to air?" she directed. "That room has not been used for so long that it needs to be well warmed. Be sure to keep the doors shut, so that the room will get warm quickly."

Connie would have liked to stay in the busy kitchen, or have stolen into the little-used front room, where there was a roaring fire now and where Cousin Cephas and Ethan Allen were sitting by the table still in their big boots, talking busily over Mr. Allen's affairs, which were also the affairs of Vermont. The spare bedroom opened off this room; for every best bedroom in a farmhouse is downstairs. There was a door from the hall into the bedroom, so that Connie could go in and out without disturbing the two men. Peter had built up the fire and she took the covers off the bed, the linen sheets, the homespun blankets, the patchwork quilt and finally even the big feather bed that served for a mattress. She hung them all on chairs before the fire so that the cold and dampness of the winter should be thoroughly driven out of them. Suddenly she heard a great burst of laughter in the kitchen. Mr. Allen had gone out to talk to Sarah and Peter. She hung the feather bed hastily over the biggest chair and ran quickly to hear what the joke was.

[111]

Mr. Ethan Allen seemed to take delight in making Sarah laugh. "You are too serious, Sarah Macomber," he said, "though I do not wonder, with all you have to think about. But do you remember—" His stories out of the past, about things that they both had seen and about people they had known, were irresistibly funny. Sarah wiped the tears of laughter from her eyes; Cousin Cephas roared; Peter chuckled and exploded and then held his breath lest he should laugh too long and miss something. Connie giggled too, until she was afraid she might not hear every word.

It was only after a long time that she suddenly remembered what she had been doing. Was the fire burning properly in their guest's room? Were the blankets near enough to it? She would run in and make sure. As she came near the door she heard odd sounds inside—Jock, what could Jock be doing? She had not noticed him for a long time.

It must be remembered that Jock was still a young dog. He had accomplished a great deal that day, and had done his duty in the cold rain as many an older farm dog might not have been so willing to do. He had lain by the fire in the kitchen until he was dry and warm, but presently he was restless and got up to prowl through the house. Any dog is aware of it, when there are unusual things going on. Jock wanted to find out all about it. Connie had left the bedroom door open. She had intended to come back at once and shut it, but she had been in such haste to hear what all the laughing was about that she never thought of it again. Jock slipped in, lay for a little while on the hearth, then began sniffing about the room, into which he had never been allowed to go. It is to be remembered again that Jock was still a young dog.

Connie came in upon him suddenly. He was having a delighted

"You are too serious, Sarah Macomber," he said.

fight with the big feather bed. He had pulled it down on the floor and was worrying it and struggling with it as puppies love to do. There were feathers all about the floor; Jock's long gray coat was full of them. He looked up at her over the edge of the great tumbled feather bed as though to say, "I had to find something to amuse myself with. So I got this. You never told me what fun feather beds were."

Connie managed to check her cry of horror. Where would Mr. Ethan Allen sleep if Jock had torn up his bed? She pushed him aside, too horrified even to scold him, and tried to discover how much harm he had done. There was one long rent in the striped cover but that seemed to be all that he had accomplished in the short time. There were feathers flying all about, but certainly there were plenty left. Sarah filled her feather beds full.

Of course she would tell Sarah afterwards, but why should she trouble her now? She was enjoying herself so much, after months of worry. Surely it would be possible to sew a patch over the place Jock had torn, and make it safe and sound again. She flew up to Sarah's room, gathered up needle and thread and scissors and cloth and came back to set to work. The kitchen was still echoing with laughter, but Connie closed her ears to it. This was something that had to be done.

A feather bed is like an enormous pillow, a very soft one. This one was much larger than Connie and it was very unmanageable. When she pressed down on it in one place it swelled out enormously in another, when she tried to move it, no matter how she tugged, it billowed and curved but did not get anywhere. When she knelt down on the edge to get at the place she wanted to sew, it went up all around her, so that she sank deep into it and almost disappeared.

[115]

She toiled away, just the same, putting in one difficult stitch after another. After she had sewed one side of the patch, she found she either had to move the feather bed or get into the very middle of it to sew in another direction. She tried both. Neither was very successful. She rolled over in the soft mass and completely disappeared. She came up again, ruffled, impatient, but absolutely determined to finish. A sound at the door caught her attention. She looked up and saw Mr. Allen standing on the threshold.

There were feathers in her own hair as well as in Jock's, and her face was red from getting down on her hands and knees, for it was only thus that she could reach her patch. She stared up at him and he stared down at her and at the same moment they both burst into laughter.

"What will you think to see your room looking like this—" she began.

"No, no," he interrupted her. "Don't grudge it to me. The sight of a woman trying to sew a patch on a feather bed is one of the best things in the world. My mother and my sisters, how they used to struggle and fight with them, and how I always loved to watch. When a woman or a girl has once sewed a patch on a feather bed she is ready to be mistress of a farm. There is nothing that takes more spirit and more patience. And you have it almost finished. I make you my compliments, Miss Constance Anderson."

When Sarah came, twenty minutes later, to make sure that the distinguished guest's room was in perfect order, she found Constance enthroned on the middle of the feather bed, discussing important matters gravely with Mr. Allen. Sarah's quick eye noted at once the neat square patch sewed on the striped ticking.

"But the winter is over now and all the hard things must be

past," Connie was saying. "And after this will every day be like every other?"

Ethan Allen shook his head. "Don't call winter over until the snow has melted before the sun, and until the water has run downhill and the streams are in their banks again. The brooks will tell you when the adventures of winter are really past. I think you are going to hear from Hebron Brook before this season is over."

IX

The Birthday Party

IT WAS on one of the early days of April that Constance stood on the doorstep and actually watched spring come. At least so it seemed. There had been four days of rain, a Thursday and Friday so stormy that none of the children could go to school, a Saturday and Sunday when the whole valley was still hidden behind the heavy dark curtain of the downpour. But early on Monday morning the weather had begun to clear, and now the storm was rolling up and up, leaving the valley visible, then the sides of the mountain and at last their bold, rocky tops. Connie saw that in those four days the spring had arrived. The long slope before her was green with new grass, the hillsides, which had been dark and gray all the winter, when they were not white, were now strange colors, faintly pink and reddish and yellow shading to green, as the trees budded and changed their dead color to a living one. A sound came up to her ears such as she had never heard before, a deep, steady, singing sound, that lifted and dropped as the puffs of warm wind carried it up the hill. "What is that?" she asked Peter, who had come out to stand beside her.

"That is Hebron Brook," he said. "The ice has broken; you will hear its voice all summer. But I have never heard it so loud as this."

When they crossed the bridge that morning Connie stopped to look down, through one of the cracks between the boards, to watch the water hurrying past. Such haste, such tumbling and foaming and leaping over the great stones in a whirl of foam! It seemed strange to stand still and quietly above it and see all that furious hurrying, hurrying, hurrying go on below her, and not hurry somewhere too. Where did it all come from, that there was always so much always hastening away to make room for more? She watched and listened till her eyes were fairly dizzy with the whirl below her, and her ears re-echoed with the sound. She could hear it still loud in her ears that night as she fell asleep. She loved it, wondered about it, listened for it. Somehow it seemed to her that she would dream of that plunging water every night forever. But she slept without dreams, as a little girl who has had a busy day is bound to do.

It was on the next afternoon, when she and Peter were turning their faces up the hill to go home from school that they heard a sound which had not come to their ears for months, the deep rumble of coach wheels on the covered bridge. The stagecoach was making its first trip of the season, and the driver on his tall seat flourished his whip in greeting. That indeed was a sign of spring.

The chickens were laying eggs fast now, the calves were impatient in the barn, and scampered and kicked up their heels when Peter let them out. How big they had grown, what fine young creatures they were. Peter walked behind them looking very old and dignified, so proud was he of what his animals had accomplished. Cousin Cephas came up to see them and he and Peter stood for a long time, leaning over the barnyard fence and talking grown-up farmer talk about this thing and that. Peter's face beamed as he came in later; evidently Cousin Cephas had praised him for what he had succeeded in doing. That was the day, too, when Connie baked a whole batch of bread by herself, a row of four beautiful, perfect loaves, that came out of the brick oven the exactly proper shade of gold shading to brown, with a fragrance that can be compared to nothing else, for freshly baked bread smells better than any other thing in the world. As least so Connie thought.

As she was studying that evening with her books spread out on the table and Peter bent over his arithmetic opposite, she found, suddenly, that the reading lesson was easy, that she could go through it without any trouble. And yet, so she remembered, she had glanced ahead at that particular lesson weeks ago and thought how fearfully hard it looked and had wondered what she would do when they came to it. And now, because she had worked so hard and tried so earnestly to read as well as the others, it was not difficult at all. Even Peter had said it was a hard lesson. Why, this meant that she could read almost as well as Peter. She had not realized how much she was learning. She sat thinking for a little while, until Peter looked across at her and grinned broadly. His face was thinner than in the autumn and his freckles had faded, although they still showed. He was taller, too, Connie noticed all of a sudden. And, how queer, she was taller herself. Last autumn she had rested her feet on the top rung of the chair as she sat to study, and now she had them on the lower one.

"What are you thinking about, Connie?" Peter asked. He did not often interrupt his lessons to speak to her, but plowed through them to the end and then tossed his book into the air with a delighted whoop. But the look of pondering on Connie's face seemed too much for him tonight and he said again, "You have an idea, Connie. What is it?"

"Why," answered Connie slowly, "I was just thinking that— that," she ended quickly, for she had found the words to it at last, "that the thing that makes spring so exciting is seeing, all of a sudden, what the winter has accomplished."

Sarah, in her chair by the fire, put down her sewing. "You are becoming a wise girl, Connie. And that is another thing that a winter on a farm brings about. People learn to think." She got up to cover the fire, for it was time for them all to go to bed. Peter closed his books and yawned. Studying had a tendency to wear Peter out, he put so much effort into it.

"Don't you think, Sarah," Constance asked as she put her papers together, "that it's almost time for the Guyer children's birthday party, for that great enormous cake you said you were going to bake?"

"I do," said Sarah promptly. "I have been thinking of it for several days. Suppose we have them come next Friday. But, mercy, I have little enough left in the storeroom after all this long winter. You must stop and ask Cousin Cephas on your way home from school if he won't bring us up some bacon and flour and sugar from the village, and let me exchange it for the wood we have left. What we got from Sam Breen wasn't enough, and we are even short of grain for the calves and chickens. And see if Margaret has any dried currants left, a birthday cake must have something gay in it. I believe the cake will just take the last flour we have."

When the Guyer children came past to go to school next day the great invitation was issued. They were dumb with astonishment at first. A birthday for all of them? Not just a birthday cake, but a birthday! Mrs. Guyer had been very good to them and gave them everything they needed, but she had never thought of their needing birthdays. Timmy let forth a high squeal of delight. They all went scampering down the hill, chattering like sparrows. The Guyer

[121]

children, too, had a message for Cousin Cephas. In their house also the food was running low. Would Cousin Cephas, as part of his duty as selectman, please see that there was some more sent to them from the village of Hebron?

They all stopped after school and told him about it. Because the cold and snow had begun so early and lasted so long, no one up here on the mountain slope had a great deal left. Cousin Cephas was going down to the village in a few days on business, and would have to be away all night, but by Saturday morning he would come back with all that they would need and would bring it up the hill on his big cart. Would that be early enough? When Connie brought back his answer Sarah nodded. Yes, that would do very well. They would be out of flour after the cake was baked, but they would have enough bread anyway and need not bake again until Saturday. But they would not have much of anything else.

It seemed like a long week, even though preparations began on Wednesday. They had to stone the currants and sift the flour and sugar and go out to find the eggs. A whole basketful of eggs it would take, but the chickens did their generous best. It was after Connie and Peter got home from school on Thursday evening that they mixed the cake. Just breaking the eggs was a task in itself. And, gracious, what a great bowl of batter Sarah had put together. Sarah stirred, Connie stirred until her arms ached, Peter stirred until even he had to confess he was too tired to lift the big wooden spoon for one more stroke, then Sarah stirred again. It was all light and yellow and fluffy at last, and was poured into the big pan which Sarah got down from the top shelf. It had indeed taken all their flour and sugar, it had practically swept the cupboard clean. It was long after bedtime when they got it into the oven. Sarah sat up to take it out when it was baked and Connie and Peter stumbled sleepily upstairs.

Next morning mild Mr. Ennis, the schoolmaster, seemed to feel that there was some unusual excitement in the air; for the whole school was quivering with it. Some of the Guyer children got their lessons far better than usual, some could not get them at all, since excitement affects different people in different ways. Connie, it had to be admitted, was very poor in hers. Only Peter kept a steady head and recited calmly and without mistakes. It was a whole hour earlier than usual when Mr. Ennis rang his bell.

"Whatever is the matter with you today, you are of no use to the world as scholars," he said. "So I think the best thing to do is just to send you all home." His eyes twinkled as he said it. Evidently he had caught the magic word as it passed from one to another and knew that this was not any usual birthday party. "And besides," he added as they filed out, "I think there is going to be rain again before evening. I want to make sure you all get home safe and dry." He stood in the doorway, watching them troop away. Connie looked back as they turned the corner of the path to cross the bridge. He was still watching, perhaps anxious to make sure that they went straight homeward and wasted no time. She waved her hand to him and he waved in return. She was to see him and know him for a long time afterwards, but she was never to see him again just as he was then, standing framed in the log doorway of the stout little schoolhouse.

There was probably not a step of real walking done all the way up to the house. As they turned into the road near the head of the bridge Cousin Cephas' wife Margaret called to them a message for Sarah and Mrs. Guyer.

"Tell them that Cephas has gone to town and will be back tomorrow with everything they need. And good luck to the birthday party."

The brownies all skipped at the very mention of the magic word and their feet went pattering over the old board floor of the bridge. Even Connie for once had scarcely time to stop even for a second to look at the white water whirling past below.

Sarah was all ready for them. On the big table in the middle of the kitchen was a pile of presents. Sarah and Connie and Peter had been making them for weeks, a wooden doll, a carved chain—for Peter was good at wood carving—a sunbonnet, a pair of knitted stockings, a gay flowered apron, a doll's patchwork quilt, treasures over which the brownies shrieked in shrill excitement and delight. Then the supper was spread with cold chicken and currant jelly, the last jar, and hot rolls—such a wealth of good things for lusty appetites. One would never have guessed that this was the final end of a long hard winter and that the shelves of the storeroom were as bare as after spring house cleaning. At last came the cake, with the room darkened and the candles lighted and the fire leaping on the hearth. Oh, what a cake! The brownies could not even squeal now, they were so full of supper and of happiness.

"Is it really ours, just for us, for our birthdays?" Tim asked, in anxious doubt.

Connie wondered what he would say if he knew that most children are used to having a birthday apiece and not a sixth share of one. But the cake was big enough to do credit to a dozen birthdays, so vast and white it was outside, so yellow and rich within. Connie had stood up to cut it and Peter was helping her to bear down upon the knife when she stopped suddenly to listen.

It was Sarah who spoke, "Hark, it's beginning to rain."

At last came the cake, with candles lighted. Oh, what a cake!

It was not merely rain, but the roar of wind, something like the voice of Hebron Brook only louder, much louder, and coming nearer and nearer. Sometimes it rose high, then it dropped to a hoarse bellow, the voice of the gale that was sweeping across the mountainside.

When people hear a storm coming they must always run quickly and do something, no matter what. Peter dashed out of the door to the barn, to make sure the calves would be safe. Connie and the brownies scurried up the stairs to fasten the wooden shutters, and Sarah rushed about below to make fast all the windows and to bar the front door. Connie, from her bedroom, could see the storm coming, a great black cloud that blotted out the valley, then the stream and the bridge, then the hillside, and suddenly was upon the house. The rain drummed and rattled against the shuttered windows, the wind rose and fell. Connie pressed her nose to a pane at the back of the house, but, although the shutter was a crack open she could see nothing but blackness outside, as though it were midnight instead of six o'clock in the afternoon. She turned back to the room. The brownies were sitting at the table, round-eyed and waiting.

Sarah had taken up the knife and was gravely cutting the next slice. "Even if the wind is high it won't spoil our cake," she declared. "Hold your plate, Tim; this slice was baked just exactly for you."

The birthday supper went on, even though the candles fluttered in the drafts, and the fire dwindled and then leaped up the chimney as the tempest rose and fell. They all ate, laughed, got up finally and played games about the kitchen. It was a gay birthday, no matter what was the darkness and noise and wind and rain outside.

"It will blow itself out," Sarah said finally. "We have only to

[127]

wait. The Guyer children will get home a little late, but Mr. and Mrs. Guyer will know where they are."

It was indeed just as Sarah had said, and the storm with a final roar swept across the hill and was gone. The rain fell less heavily and finally stopped. Connie opened a window and the fresh, sweet, wet smell of spring came in, and with it a new sound.

"That's Hebron Brook," Peter said beside her, tugging at the shutter fastening. "Did you ever hear it sound so loud?"

No, not even Sarah had ever heard the brook roar like that.

The clouds were carried clean away and the sky was clear, with stars coming out. Sarah lighted the lantern and they all put on their cloaks. She and Connie and Peter were going to see the brownies home. As they climbed the hill they saw the marks of wind every-where, great branches snapped off the butternut trees, twigs strew-ing the ground, places indeed where the path was still deep in running water and they had to scramble over the rocks at the sides. At the Guyer house, which was so high up the hill that it had been even harder struck by the storm, the pigpen had been blown over but, fortunately, not before the pig family had been safely driven into the barn. But there was a whole dozen of round spotted pig babies who had been soaked and chilled and were being warmed before the fire in the summer kitchen. Mr. Guyer, an old man, went limping about giving directions, lamenting and worrying. Mrs. Guyer was calmer, but she looked anxious and tired.

"I'm glad the storm passed quickly," she said. "I hope it won't interfere with Cephas getting back from the village with all the things we need. I'm blessed if I have more than three meals worth more in the cupboard. I've never known a winter to last so long."

The three came down the hill again. The night was growing

lighter, for the moon was coming up. The path was difficult to follow, in some places it was quite washed away. A tiny stream, which usually came trickling and murmuring down beside the path, was now a plunging brook, pouring over its stones, sweeping around curves with a loud tumult of hurrying waters.

"Let's go down the lane," Constance proposed as they came near their own house. "I want to see how the water is in Hebron Brook."

Even from there it was possible to hear with what a new voice the brook was shouting below. It sounded angry now instead of being loud and hurried as they had heard it for days. The others wanted to see it as much as Connie, so they walked onward down the hill, the moon above them growing brighter and brighter as they went.

Not one of them was prepared for what they saw when they reached Hebron Brook. Sarah herself had never known such a thing in all the years she had lived on the mountain and Hebron Brook had flowed under the covered bridge. It was beaten into yellow foam and was rolling in great heaving waves that went pouring down the bed of the stream. The water was so high it filled the whole rocky bed; the water had come up and up, so that the wide tossing level of beaten foam was almost on a level with the floor of the bridge. Branches and whole trees, torn up by the roots further above, came drifting down and caught against the beams; for the stream was so high that they could not pass beneath. A great muddy tangle began to gather and hang against the upper wall of the bridge. It grew larger and larger even as they watched.

They stood staring until Peter said, speaking loud to be heard above the noisy water, "The stream has risen even since we were standing here. It is going to be over the floor of the bridge in a very little while."

"But what will all the sticks and tree trunks do?" Connie asked. "They can't float away."

Sarah spoke, raising her voice as Peter had done. "They will carry the bridge away. See how they are battering against it now. If the water comes up even a few inches more, they will sweep the bridge downstream, boards and beams and everything together. There is nothing that can save it."

"There must be," Peter cried. "There has to be a way to save it."

Sarah answered hopelessly, "Once, a long time ago, my husband saw some such thing was going to happen and he went out to the middle and knocked off some of the boards, to make a place for the water to sweep through. He knew it in time, and he managed to save it. But it is too late for anything like that now."

The water began to rise more quickly. Peter stood thinking and staring in the moonlight, saying nothing. Then suddenly he exclaimed in a hard, clear voice that was almost like a man's, "It's not too late." He turned away and went dashing up the hill.

"Peter, come back," Sarah cried. "There's nothing you can do now."

Even Connie felt that it was hopeless. But she stood there, watching, unable to take her eyes away. To see the bridge shiver into pieces and go whirling downstream, what a strange, what a terrible sight. If Cousin Cephas were there, could he have done anything? Perhaps not. And Cousin Cephas was far away. Had Peter gone to call old Mr. Guyer? He could scarcely be of any help. But Peter was back, even as she began to wonder. He carried a coil of rope, a crow bar, the ax from the woodblock and the little sharp hatchet.

"You can help, Connie," he said. "There isn't much danger for a minute or two yet." He ran out on the bridge to the middle. Sarah did not protest, but followed him with Connie close beside. Constance was afraid Sarah would order them back, but she did not. The look on her face was exactly like the look on Peter's. They would both dare anything to save the covered bridge.

X

Hebron Brook

PETER, CONSTANCE and Sarah all worked together desperately, and as though they were one person. The voice of the waters made a queer hollow echoing as they stood in the tunnel of the bridge, very different from the wild free sound they listened to outside. It was Sarah who gave directions, for she had seen the bridge saved once and knew what must be done now that it was threatened again. But it was Peter who was sure that they could save it.

"Take the lower side, the wall that faces downstream," Sarah directed. "It will be easy to knock a hole in the boards there, then we can try the other."

A bridge that has stood twenty years, and is built to stand a hundred more, is hard to tear to pieces. But Ethan Allen had made an opening in it once, and Peter could do it again. And if human hands could save it, saved it should be.

Peter chopped, with great swinging blows of the ax, trying to cut through the big wooden pins which held the wall boards in place on the downstream side. Connie was chopping too with the hatchet. Whenever a board cracked under Peter's ax he would move forward and leave her and Sarah to thrust the iron bar under it and wrench it free. One plank gave way and then another. Peter climbed up a slanting beam, steadied himself on one of the cross timbers and knocked the boards free at the top. They dropped one by one and

[132]

were whirled away like matches, leaving a great gaping hole on the lower side.

"Now the other." Peter was breathless now, as he climbed down and turned to strike with all his might at the opposite wall. He chopped steadily, never wildly, knowing just where each blow should be put. There was a loud crack, and another, the boards were giving way. But the task was no easy one, the very force of the water held the planks in place. Peter chopped, the other two strained and struggled. Connie felt something cold about her feet and looked down to see that the water was trickling over the floor.

Peter had stopped to draw a breath. "They are free at the bottom, I have to climb up now and knock them off at the top." He looked down at the water coming up around their feet and said steadily, "There's still time, there's plenty of time."

Sarah nodded. It still could be done if he were quick. Sarah took Constance firmly by the hand and led her toward the shore. "We can't help him now," she said.

She still held Connie's hand as they turned about to watch. Just as they stepped off the bridge a deep ripple washed over it and wet Connie's ankles, but she scarcely felt it.

How she wished she were Peter, as he scrambled up a beam, braced himself on two cross timbers and began to swing his ax. "Crack, crack, crack," it sounded above the roar of the water. The instant the boards were loosened the stream began to snatch at them; they fell one after another and went whirling away. There was a wide opening and the brook was running through, a foaming torrent all across the floor where they had just been standing, and with Peter bold and triumphant perched on the strong framework above. He left the ax on a beam and came scrambling toward them. Connie could see how he was grinning with relief and she heard Sarah breathe a "Thank God" that was almost a sob. He had almost reached the shore, and was climbing down, when his hand slipped and he fell. A curl of water came washing all around him. He struggled for a second. It was Connie, holding to a beam and catching at his arm, who held him firm, so that he got to his feet, and came splashing to dry ground.

They all stood watching for a minute, fifteen minutes, half an hour. Was it true that the water had dropped a little? It had. The bridge had been a dam, an obstacle that the stream would not endure. Now that its waters could run free again, the stream spread out to flow more smoothly and evenly. It was not angry now. Hebron Brook was no longer determined to destroy the covered bridge.

For a long time the three could not drag themselves away. It was as though a spell were upon them and as though the bridge was only safe as long as they watched it, black and clear in the moonlight, with the water glittering silver as it flowed over the floor. Then at last Sarah spoke sharply.

"Why in the world do we stand here gaping, and Peter wet through?" They turned and went up the hill, but Connie looked back again and again to make sure, absolutely sure, that the bridge was still standing.

They opened the door of the house and went in, all of them wet, Peter still dripping. Connie stopped in surprise. It seemed so long ago that they had left it, that she hardly knew what this thing meant, the big, half-cut cake on the table and the burnt-out candles. Peter cut himself a slice and ate it. Sarah was building up the fire.

"It is good that we all like birthday cake," she observed. "There's very little else we'll have to eat in this house until Cephas comes up to us. And if the bridge had gone, heaven only knows when we would have got anything, either for ourselves or the poor beasts in the barn. But the water will go down now, and Cephas will get to us before tomorrow is over. Now drink a cup of hot milk, both of you, and get to your beds."

When Connie came downstairs next morning, Sarah was making milk porridge before the fire, but Peter had gone out first to see to the calves and then to race down the hill to look at Hebron Brook. It was running more quietly, he reported, although the floor of the bridge was still flooded. The bridge was standing safe.

"We could get to school if the water is only as deep as that," Peter suggested conscientiously, but he grinned at Sarah's prompt answer:

"I may let you wade in ice-cold water when I must, but once in twenty-four hours is enough, I think. Sit down and eat your porridge now. We're not in any real danger of starving, but I'll be glad when Cephas comes. And there's still some birthday cake."

People have a way of feeling hungrier than usual when there is not much food in sight. Connie felt that she could have eaten two breakfasts the size of that one, and that birthday cake in the morning was rather surprising fare. There was some skimmed milk to give to the chickens. As for the calves, there was a little new grass for them to nibble, although it was not long enough for them to get more than one good bite of a tuft here and there that had grown tall in the sun. But they were delighted to be let loose, to run and kick and jump into the air until it made Constance laugh aloud to watch them.

Sarah seemed to be pondering as to how to make the most of this day when Connie was free from school. "I've certainly precious little cooking to do," she observed. "Of course we could do some . house cleaning, but there, the first days of spring come and go so quickly and are like nothing else in the world. Suppose we go up the hill to look for wild flowers. The hepaticas will be out."

They went up the long slope, all three together, with Jock galloping ahead. The little hill brook was pouring down noisily. They crossed it on stepping stones. How warm the sun felt on their backs and how bright the sky was! Little yellow flowers were showing here and there in the grass, and even the silvery green cushions of mullein leaves were beginning to appear. They came to where a spur of woods stretched out into the pasture. There was no snow between the big trunks now, but the wood was clean and open with the bushes bare and the twisting vines still leafless. Some little red berries of wintergreen were left from last autumn, among the delicate green tufts of new moss.

At first Connie could not see any flowers, but Sarah told her to look again. Then she began to catch sight of them in the open places where the sun fell warm and clear, making bright patches on the dark leaves. There, opening to the warmth and brightness, were the hepatica flowers, their bluish-white cups spreading wide to let the sunshine into their very hearts, their dark brittle leaves brown among the brown of those which had fallen from the maple trees to keep them warm all winter. Connie began picking them, coming across frail pointed blood-root flowers here and there also, but everywhere discovering more and more of the pale, delicate blossoms of the hepaticas. She had a great bunch presently, and so had Sarah, when Peter told them firmly that it was past noon and they must go home.

"He wants to explain to the calves why they aren't getting any grain today," Sarah declared.

[136]

How warm the sun felt on their backs and how bright the sky was!

Constance came slowly down the slope, looking at all the green and blue and the brightness everywhere about her. The floor of the valley was spread below her feet; the squares of the fields were all different shades and colors, where they had been plowed or planted or where the green of new grass was covering the pasture lots. The mountains looked big and near; the blue of the distant ones was deep and brilliant, cutting sharply into the paler blue of the sky. Faintly, very faintly, there came up to her ears, even here, the song of Hebron Brook. She stood still, looking and looking, not thinking, but only feeling. If her half-finished thoughts could possibly have been put into words it would have been something like this—

"What a pity it is that all the people in the world don't know how beautiful it is just here." And this was what living on a farm was, all this work, all these adventures, all this beauty. What a great deal for just four words to say, "Living on a farm." But she would always know what they really meant.

They came into the house and Sarah managed to get a few things together so that they sat down to something like a meal. "We won't have many dishes to wash," Peter suggested cheerfully.

But Sarah's face was grave and she said more than once, "Mrs. Guyer said she had three meals left, didn't she? Then the brownies aren't hungry yet. I wish Cephas would come."

After the work was all done, Constance sat down in the big cushioned chair in a bright pool of sunshine beside the window. She was pleasantly sleepy and so comfortable. How much they had done the night before, how late they had all been up! Why, it must have been— Her eyes closed. She was awakened by the creak of wheels and by the sound of Sarah's flinging open the door and exclaiming, "Cephas, God bless vou. How good that you are here."

[139]

Connie ran out to see Cousin Cephas with the big cart and the pair of black and white oxen. A heavy task it was even for them, to pull that laden cart up the hill; for it was piled high with sacks of flour and sugar, with sides of bacon and bags of coffee. It looked as though no one could be hungry for a year with all that food unloaded at the door.

Peter helped to lift down the bags and bundles, and Sarah and Connie carried them in to set them on the storeroom shelves. What a different feeling it gave one to see the place piled up with supplies again, a safe, happy, powerful feeling as though there would never be need to be anxious about anything again. Then Peter and Cousin Cephas and the oxen went creaking off up the hill to carry the Guyers their share. Presently they came down again and loaded the cart with wood, of which Sarah still had a greater pile than she needed, and then Cousin Cephas suggested to Connie. "Perhaps you would like to come down with us and see what the storm has done. It's going to surprise you."

Had something happened to the bridge after all? Connie wondered in a second of panic. But no, that couldn't be, or Cousin Cephas would not have got up to them. They went down all together, the oxen, with their big careful feet, stepping sedately down the lane, Peter driving them as he loved to do, holding a stick before their noses to signal whether they were to go slowly or faster, saying "Gee" and "Haw" when they were to turn right or left. As they came near the brook Cousin Cephas declared that the water had fallen even since he came up the hill. Was it really only last night that they had fought with the angry stream and kept it from devouring the bridge? The water was flowing now, in thin, clear ripples across the floor, not half an inch deep. Jock went rushing

[140]

through it, throwing out a great spray on each side. Peter and Cousin Cephas splashed across, dry in their big boots; the oxen trod cautiously but seemed rather to like it. Connie rode over on the cart.

"Now," said Cousin Cephas suddenly as they halted on the other side. "Just look there at the schoolhouse."

"But what's happened," Connie cried. "It isn't there."

A pile of boards and logs and broken window frames was all that was left of the schoolhouse. A few hours ago Mr. Ennis was standing in the door, wishing them good luck for the birthday, and now he could never stand just there again. He was safe in his own house when the storm broke. It was the wind, and not Hebron Brook which had brought the building down. It was just as well that they had all gone home early to the birthday party.

"But where will we go to school now?" Connie asked blankly.

"School's very nearly over," Cousin Cephas told her. "Here in the country it has to end early so that the children can help with the spring planting. That's a time when a farm needs every pair of hands it can get. And I've been thinking that, since more than half of you live up the hill, you might as well have school in Sarah's big kitchen if she's of a mind to let you."

They went on to Cousin Cephas' barnyard where he and Peter unloaded the wood and piled the cart with a great mound of hay which Cousin Cephas had thrown down from the loft. "The cattle have been in the barn too much this long winter and I'm going to turn them out. They're wild to get to the new grass. There isn't quite enough to feed them yet, but I'm taking up some loads of hay so they won't go hungry."

Therefore when they went out of the gate and rumbled across the bridge again, there was a long procession trailing out behind them.

[141]

Nicodemus the great bull walked just behind, his big black head so close to Connie's knee, as she sat in the back of the cart, that she could reach out and pat him when the oxen went slower. Behind him came the cows, the nearly grown calves, the whole herd trudging quietly and properly behind the big leader.

But when they had mounted the hill, when Peter and Cousin Cephas had let down the pasture bars to turn the cattle in on the new grass, what running there was, what flirting of heels, what tossing of black heads and rolling of great eyes, what rocking-horse galloping across the slopes. Jock ran and barked and swung them this way and that. He was a very proud dog now, this was his real duty, this was the herd which would be under his charge as long as he could drive cattle. The calves raced and skipped sideways, even Nicodemus dropped his head and began pawing the ground in his excitement. Then they all scattered over the hill, snatching mouthfuls of grass, looking and snuffing here and there, exploring their old feeding ground, glad beyond the power of dumb beasts' telling, to be out on the free, wild mountain again.

Connie sat on the edge of the cart thinking how gay and strong and happy they were until suddenly Cousin Cephas' voice broke in upon her.

"I declare, I clean forgot to give you your letter. The coach couldn't get over the bridge yesterday and so left your mail at my house. I've had it in my pocket for you since I set out up the hill."

Constance took it slowly and broke the seal. She was always slow with letters from her father and mother, to make them last longer. She read—how easily she could read now—and suddenly was slow no more. Her eyes raced down the page hardly taking in the words, news of a ship coming in, of a long voyage ended, of dear ones coming home at last. The final words, above her father's name, said:

"I'm coming up to get you by the first coach I can manage to take."

She jumped down from the cart. Oxen were not fast enough to carry a little girl with such news within her.

"Sarah," she shouted even when she was a long way off, "Sarah, they've come home again. He's coming for me."

She stood still, having got the words out, and waited until Peter, with a very sober face, came tramping up the hill. "Did you hear, Peter? Aren't you glad?"

"Yes, I'm glad," he agreed, "but—you will go away, Connie."

That was true, she would go away. All that glorious broad valley, that long mountain slope, the low house against the side of the hill, the pasture and the cattle dotted over it, Sarah's dear kind face, Peter's slow smile, when would she ever see them again?

Her voice sounded choked as she said, "Yes, Peter, I'm going away, but surely you and Sarah will let me come back."

Peter's serious face brightened into his own glad smile. "Oh, Connie, think what fun to see the coach stop and watch you jump out and come running up the hill. Promise me that you will surely come. Cousin Cephas is going to buy two of the calves, but the other one will be full grown then and we will have our own crop of corn and apples." He and Sarah were never going to leave the farm now, it was theirs to keep and to make prosper for the rest of their lives.

A few days went by, while the bright spring seemed to grow warmer and greener almost with every hour. They did indeed have school in Sarah's big kitchen, with the brownies sitting in rows on the new benches and Sarah coming in with a big pitcher of milk and a mountain of cookies, "just to break up the long morning." Mr. Ennis seemed to be quite as glad to have it broken as any of the rest of them.

The schoolmaster had saved a few things from the wreck of the schoolhouse, one of them being the big map which hung now upon Sarah's wall. On the last morning Connie stood up before them all and traced on it the course of her father's ship north from the West Indies, homeward bound.

It was the very next afternoon that the coach stopped below the hill and the guard blew his horn, with that deep sweet note that meant someone was arriving. As Connie rushed out to see, there was a tall figure striding up the hill, a broad-shouldered man with a sunburned face and with his arms stretched wide for Connie to run into them. It was her father.

The coach would not come back for two days, two beautiful days in which she could show him everything, tell him all about everything, while Sarah watched them both with her quietly happy face that reflected the joy on Connie's.

"Yes, we've made a good winter of it," Constance heard her telling Captain Anderson. "We've taken care of the farm between us and we know that we can go on with it. Peter and I can manage, we are certain of that now. I will be getting older all the time, to be sure, but then, so will he. But I don't know how we could have succeeded, either of us, in this hard winter without Constance to help. She will surely come back to us another year, in the summer. You must promise that she will."

The moment for going came, the carpet bag was packed, the coach came rolling up and stopped for them to climb in. The horses started; their hoofs sounded hollow on the covered bridge and the walls echoed the sound of the wheels.

"That's the hole Peter made," Connie told her father as they rumbled through. Long slivers of sunlight fell through the cracks in the wall, ran across Connie's face. She was leaning out, so that as soon as they were clear of the bridge she could look back up the hill. There they were above, Sarah waving her apron, Peter standing so tall beside her, both arms lifted in a last signal of good-by. He was bigger and broader than the old Peter, but his dark figure against the sky looked once more like the Peter on the wall of the kitchen where Connie first heard about him, like the Peter printed on the snow she had seen on the night of her coming.

Cousin Cephas was at his gate to wave his hat and there at the next crossroads was a tall figure on a big black horse, both splashed with mud.

"Look, look!" she cried to her father. "It's Mr. Ethan Allen."

Not many little girls could have one of the great men of America's history to wave her good-by. A mile further and she saw a little gray house on a hillside, with a plowed field below it and a tall youth going back and forth sowing grain. That must be Dick McGowan, he had come up the hill once to show Peter the colt he had bought. He stopped to shade his eyes and watch the coach roll by.

Yes, certainly she would come back to all this. She settled back on the seat with a happy sigh. You could always think about coming back to a farm. That was the last beautiful thing to think about, that the valley and the mountains and the long slope of the hill would always be there, would always be the same.

Date Du